THE
FIVE WONDERS
OF
THE DANUBE

Zoran Živković

The Five Wonders of the Danube
Copyright © 2011 by Zoran Živković

FG-RS0007L3
ISBN: 978-4-908793-25-7

Cover: Youchan Ito, Togoru Art Works

Neoclassic Fleurons font used with permission of
Paulo W–Intellecta Design

Cadmus Press
cadmusmedia.org

THE FIVE WONDERS OF THE DANUBE

Zoran Živković

Translated from the Serbian
by
Alice Copple-Tošić

Cadmus Press
2017

Contents

First Wonder
Black Bridge, Regensburg

THE PAINTING WAS FOUND on the Black Bridge in Regensburg on Sunday at 06:12.

Although large (243 × 171 centimeters, as it was later established), it could have passed unnoticed at that early hour. The guard making his first round was interested in the lower parts of the bridge. Birds alone had access to the upper parts and they posed no threat. They fouled the metal and stone, but that was not part of his responsibility.

He didn't like the river gulls because of their filth and—even more—because their shrieking jangled his nerves. But if their cries hadn't suddenly resounded, he would certainly have missed the painting. Just as he reached the middle of the bridge, they began to shriek. He raised his eyes and was doubly amazed.

The mysterious appearance of the painting should have been the greater surprise, of course, but what primarily astonished the guard was the gulls' unexpected agitation. They usually stood on the bridge's tall railing, but not one was there now. A dozen birds were circling low and shrieking so insufferably that he would have covered his ears with his hands had he not been on duty.

When the painting finally caught his attention, once again a further consideration prevailed. His first thought was of what awaited him when he reported to his supervisor at the District Bridge Administration. He would certainly be accused of sleeping in the guard-house and such an offence would have to be severely punished. He might even lose his job. It would do no good to swear that he hadn't had a wink of sleep all night long. The fact that he had not fallen asleep in the thirty-seven years he'd been on the job would also be of no help. He could almost hear his supervisor's thundering voice: "If you were awake, how could someone have hung such a big painting on top of the bridge?"

He had no answer to that question. How, indeed? And without being heard or seen? At least, he hadn't heard or seen anything. The bridge was illuminated and there'd been almost no traffic that night. In any case, no one had stopped. And this couldn't have been the work of just one person. One tall ladder wouldn't have been enough, plus tools would be needed to attach the painting. There were no hooks up above from which to hang it.

Then there was the question of why anyone would do such a thing. Who hangs paintings on bridges? True enough, river crossings attracted various eccentrics—hadn't he met a few of them over the years?—but they were always crazy loners, and this would have required the work of several people. Was it some sort of plot? Fear filled the guard. What if it was a political stunt? Then he would be in even greater trouble. He would naturally fall under suspicion as an accessory. Not only would he lose his job, he'd end up in jail.

He threw back his head and stared anxiously at the large unframed canvas as though suddenly realizing that something was painted on it. The foreground showed the downstream side of the bridge, the side on which it was placed. The scene beyond the railing on the canvas was the same as that beyond the real railing: the meandering course of the river through a plain to the distant hills in the east where the sun had recently risen. Looking past the painting, the guard squinted at the sun which hung in the same place as on the canvas. The painting seemed to invoke this very moment, an impression that was reinforced by the flock of river gulls flying in all directions. They were depicted so faithfully that it seemed the shrieking was coming from the painting too.

He felt a little better. Nothing on the painting was politically incorrect. At least he wouldn't be accused of taking part in a conspiracy. Other motives were behind this. He didn't even try to grasp what they might be. What did they have to do with him, anyway? It could be the teamwork of madmen or jokers, it made no difference. Let those who were in charge take care of it. All that interested him was how they'd done it. He would have to answer to his superiors for that. And what could he tell them? That he had no idea? How nice. Something as serious as this happens on the bridge he's guarding and he's unable to offer any explanation.

He was suddenly struck by an idea that seemed to be a life-saver. Indeed, this would be the first time he breached the regulations that required he report every unusual incident, but now that would be the lesser of two evils. He would get out of trouble by removing its cause. No one else had seen the painting. If he managed to take it down and hide it, no one would be the wiser. The best thing would be to drop it into the river. Then no trace would be left. The water would quickly wash the paint off the canvas and turn it into an ordinary rag.

The guard's conscience pricked him. What a shame, it was such a pretty painting. Perhaps he could keep it. He wouldn't take the risk of having it framed and had no wall large enough to hang it on in his small apartment, but he would keep it rolled up under his bed and take it out from time to time to look at it. Particularly after his upcoming retirement. It would be a pleasant memento of all the years he'd worked there. The guardhouse where he'd spent almost one-third of his life could also be seen at the edge of the painting.

He was not without mementos. Above his bed were three rows of photographs taken from the bridge, thirty-seven in all—one for each year of service. He appeared in them too and liked to look at them, following them back as he got younger and younger and the snapshots faded. He was not in the painting, however, but this was a work of art. How many guards could boast of having a painting of the bridge where they worked, particularly one as big as this?

Yes, but how was he going to get it down? He would have trouble doing it by himself and didn't possess a ladder tall enough. As he feverishly considered all the difficult and unfeasible ways of reaching the top of the railing without a ladder—at which point he would see how to deal with the canvas—the inevitable happened. A car headed across the bridge. Catching sight of the guard standing in the middle looking up at something, the driver's curiosity got the better of him. He stopped and stuck his head out of the window.

The guard turned around and motioned angrily at the driver to move on, then headed for the guardhouse at the end of the bridge to make a call. He no longer had a choice. It was pointless to remove the painting now that someone else had seen it. He would have to make an official report of the incident. That might be better after all. Losing your job hardly compared with losing your life while climbing up the bridge's metal superstructure. In any case, memories should be personal. If he'd been in the painting, he might have taken the foolhardy risk.

2

THE GUARDHOUSE WAS CRAMPED under the best of circumstances and now there was no room at all. Had his supervisor been thinner, it would have seemed roomier, but he must have weighed at least one hundred and twenty-five kilos. The solitary chair creaked ominously when his hulking body fell into it. Even if there'd been another chair, the guard would have stayed on his feet.

His supervisor did not go to the middle of the bridge to examine the painting up close. What interested him first and foremost could be seen from the end. He eyed it and confirmed that it was truly as big as he'd been told, then went into the guardhouse. Even though he'd arrived in an official black car, his face was flushed. He was always out of breath when he had to get dressed at short notice.

As the guard had anticipated, after three brief preliminary questions he was asked the one that he couldn't answer: "If you were awake, how did someone put such a large painting on top of the bridge?" All he did was shrug his shoulders helplessly and bow his head.

Only the supervisor's heavy breathing disturbed the strained silence that filled the guardhouse.

"Let's be matter-of-fact," he growled at last. "The world is rationally ordered. Or perhaps you feel otherwise?"

The guard briskly shook his bowed head.

"Then it's clear to you that the painting didn't get there by itself."

This time his head nodded, but remained lowered.

"Let's see what rational explanations we have available. First, you fell asleep. . ."

The supervisor raised a fat hand when the guard opened his mouth to protest.

"I know, I know. You claim you didn't. That claim might not even be false. That is, you are convinced that you didn't fall asleep when you actually did, but don't remember. Forgetfulness is not unusual late in life. How old are you?"

"Fifty-seven." He finally raised his head because he was able to give an incontestable answer.

"There, you see. Have you thought of early retirement?"

"I have just three years until full retirement. . . ." he replied softly.

"A lot of thorny situations can materialize during three years in the difficult service of guarding a bridge. I recommend you give serious thought to retiring soon."

The supervisor looked the guard in the eye until he briefly nodded.

"Very good. Let's continue. Are you interested in painting, by any chance?"

"Painting?" repeated the guard in surprise. "I haven't any talent for that."

"That would not stop you. Most of the people who paint have no talent. Their biggest problem is where to exhibit their daubs. The galleries won't have them, of course, so they are ready to put them up just about anywhere so they can be seen. And why not on bridges? A lot of people go across them."

"But that painting," said the guard, motioning toward the middle of the bridge, "is not a daub. It's very . . . faithful. It could be shown in the best galleries."

"Isn't that what you would say if it were yours?"

"It isn't mine. I assure you. If you would just look . . ."

"I will. After we consider the third possibility. The painting is quite big, right?"

"Big. . . ."

"Regardless of who painted it, they couldn't have put it up there by themselves."

"No, they couldn't."

"They had to have help. An accomplice."

"They must have. . . ."

"Not only to put it up but . . . Guess what else?"

The guard stared at his supervisor for a few moments in silence, then shook his head.

"I can't."

"But it's simple. The biggest obstacle to carrying out their intention would be the bridge guard. The vigilant, attentive and conscientious guard. There are two ways to take care of him. Incapacitate him, which is not very advisable since this would be a serious crime. Attacking an official in the course of his duties. You'd go to prison for that. It would be much more expedient to win him over. Not all guards are honest, unfortunately. For a tidy sum, there are those who'd pretend they hadn't seen a thing. The smarter ones would admit contritely that they'd fallen asleep. That's an offence, but it's less than being an accomplice. Those who weren't as bright would persistently repeat that they hadn't slept and simply had no explanation for how the painting got to the top of the bridge."

The guard squinted. "I swear. . . ."

"Now is not the time for swearing. We'll deal with that later. Right now we have more important business. We can't leave the painting up there. It has to be taken down as soon as possible. Let's go."

The chair creaked once more in relief as the bulky mass set it free. When the supervisor left the guard-house, he didn't walk toward the middle of the bridge even though it was only eighty-one meters away. He sat in the car and ordered the driver to take him. The guard, who, naturally, was not invited, hastened in the same direction with long strides. Were it not for his complete distraction, he might have noticed that the irritating sounds had disappeared. As it was, he covered a good two-thirds of the distance before finally realizing there wasn't a single river gull in the sky. They weren't on the bridge railing either. They'd flown off somewhere.

He approached his supervisor timidly and stood at attention in front of him, although regulations did not require it. A touch of humility wouldn't hurt. He said not a word lest he disturb his superior standing there staring at the painting. He waited patiently to be addressed.

"You didn't paint this," said the supervisor at last.

The guard felt a great sense of relief. Despite the steadfastly severe voice, at least one doubt had been removed.

"No, I didn't," he hastened to confirm, raising his eyes to the painting. "I would never be able . . ."

His superior failed to note that the sentence was left

unfinished. Since he was still looking up, he didn't observe, either, how his subordinate's eyes had widened.

"Go back to the guardhouse," he ordered sharply. "You aren't needed here. We'll continue our conversation later."

The guard hesitated briefly, then gave a curt nod and clicked his heels like a good soldier receiving an order. He turned around and headed for the end of the bridge.

It was best this way, he concluded. He wouldn't say anything. Why should he worsen his otherwise unenviable position? All he needed was for them to declare him insane. What could he do to corroborate his words? Indeed, there was an eyewitness, but how could he find him? And even if he found him, who would believe them? No one, of course. As his supervisor had wisely reminded him, the world has a rational order. One painting can't turn into another.

~ 3 ~

ALTHOUGH IT MIGHT NOT seem so at first glance, the supervisor was an art lover. Considering the work he did, it was not surprising that he was particularly attracted to works about bridges. He collected everything related to them: prose, poetry and plays, all types of music, paintings of various sizes and techniques. The walls of his large office at the District Bridge Administration belonged to the arts: they were covered with framed paintings and shelves full of books and records.

The supervisor was proud of his collection, but there was something that slightly clouded his pleasure. While he considered his books and records to be originals, he was painfully aware that the paintings were only reproductions. It could not have been otherwise.

Although he didn't complain about his income, it was quite insufficient to buy original paintings. He couldn't ask the State Bridge Administration for help, of course. Bureaucrats without the slightest feeling for art worked there. One day, perhaps, if he was promoted in the service, as he hoped . . .

But when he'd raised his eyes this morning to the canvas that someone had placed on the bridge, his very first thought was that lady luck had smiled on him. Here was a chance finally to get hold of an excellent original—and at no cost. The supervisor had absolutely no doubts about it being an original, and a new one at that. He was very well acquainted with paintings of bridges and there were none among them—particularly not of this size—that would make this a reproduction.

In addition, a cursory glance was enough to determine that this was not the work of an amateur but the canvas of a true master. The supervisor had just started examining it in greater detail, trying to figure out who might be the artist, when the guard approached. Although he hadn't deigned to look at him, he'd felt the little man go rigid. He couldn't concentrate properly with him standing there, so he'd quickly sent him back to the guardhouse. That was where he belonged, anyway.

He spent several more minutes examining it carefully, but got nowhere near to solving the mystery. Certain details led him to think of three possible painters, but not one of them was Austrian. Of course, Austrian painters weren't the only ones who painted Austrian bridges, but that was what naturally came to mind.

He envied the Viennese their bridges. Not so much for their beauty—German bridge builders lagged not in the least behind the Austrians; on the contrary—but for their size. Bridges have to be beautiful, of course, but if they aren't big then beauty alone doesn't count for much. And the size of the bridge depends on the size of the river. In the Regensburg district, where he was in charge, the Danube was quite narrow, but in Vienna it was a real, wide river.

Recognizing at once the famous Yellow Bridge, although presented from a bird's-eye view, the supervisor concluded with a smile that he was really in luck. It was truly remarkable that no one had painted the prettiest bridge in Vienna before. Now he alone would have a painting of it, and an original one at that, not a mere reproduction.

He started thinking about the best place to put it in his office. There was almost no room on the walls, but that was no problem. He would take down as many reproductions as necessary. Despite the fact that he'd been a passionate collector, getting rid of them would be no trouble. They were just copies after all. Only an original was unique.

The rapture that filled him had blocked out questions he had to ask himself—by virtue of his profession if not his curiosity. First of all, how did the painting get on the bridge? And then, did he dare keep it?

The first question didn't worry him very much. He would have liked to know the answer but it really made no difference how the canvas got there. The world was full of oddballs, but why go to the trouble of finding out why they'd decided to bring this big painting here of all places? And such investigations were not part of his job description. In any case, if someone should lose sleep over it, it was the guard.

The second question was far more pertinent. Strictly speaking, he didn't have the right to keep someone else's property. Yes, but to whom did the canvas belong? If it had been a well-known painting stolen from a museum or gallery, he clearly would not even think of taking it. But this was obviously a new work. Perhaps it had been stolen from the artist—whoever he was—just after it was finished? There were more malicious and jealous people in the world than eccentrics. In that case the supervisor could only expect gratitude for keeping it safe in his office. And what if no one came looking for the painting? That could not be excluded either. What if the artist himself had put it here and didn't care what happened to it? Artists were the greatest eccentrics of all.

In any case, the best thing would be to get the canvas down as soon as possible and take it to his office. Fortunately, it was still early so everything could be done inconspicuously, without witnesses, before the police got wind of the puzzling event on the bridge. They alone could spoil his plans. Then the painting would end up in the police depot and not with him.

He shuddered at the thought. Hesitating briefly as to whether to take the car again or go on foot, he headed for the guardhouse with strides as brisk as his weight would allow. Even though he'd be out of breath again, this way was faster. He wasted too much time getting into the car and particularly getting out of it.

As he advanced it crossed his mind that there would be unwanted witnesses nevertheless: first the guard and then the workers he would call from the guardhouse to come and take down the painting. This wasn't too worrisome, however. He had an effective way of ensuring their silence. Long ago he'd seen for himself what could be achieved by offering the possibility of dismissal or promotion.

∽ 4 ∾

Workers were brought by truck to the Black Bridge in seventeen minutes. The supervisor was undecided what to do until they got there. He didn't feel like staying in the guardhouse. Indeed, the guard had politely gone outside as soon as he'd reached for the phone, but he felt uncomfortable inside even without him. The guardhouse had not been built to his standards and not only because it was cramped.

As he stood in front of the guardhouse, he noticed that his driver had brought the car back to the end of the bridge. The driver got out and opened the back door, but the supervisor only waved his hand in refusal. Whenever he had the choice, he preferred to sit rather than stand, but now a bit more walking would do him good. This would satisfy his doctor who kept reminding him that he had to get more exercise.

He headed back to the middle of the bridge, but soon stopped and turned around. Words were not necessary. All he had to do was scowl at the guard for him to understand that no escort was wanted. Bowing his head, the guard went back to the guardhouse and stood in front of it, clearly not knowing what else to do.

When the supervisor got below the painting, he didn't look up at it again. He would have had to hold his head thrown way back and his cervical vertebrae had already started some serious ossification. He would be able to enjoy the painting from a better angle soon, when it was on the wall opposite his desk. His eyes wandered downstream through the railing.

As he stood there, something crossed his mind. Ever since he'd become a supervisor at the District Administration, he'd mostly seen bridges on the reproductions that surrounded him in his office. There was no need to go to real bridges except in unusual circumstances such as this, and fortunately they were rare. As far as he could recall, the last time he'd been on a bridge was a good two months ago, and it had been much longer since he'd stood idly like this on one of them. In his younger days he'd enjoyed walking across bridges and looking down at the river, but this affinity had gotten lost somewhere. Perhaps because he truly did not get enough exercise.

The river gulls attracted his attention all at once. From the outset he'd been vaguely aware that birds were floating on the water's surface, but there was no reason to focus on them. They were a common enough sight. Now, however, they suddenly became uncommon. The combination of the gulls' random movements and the river current had resulted in a dozen feathered floaters forming a rectangle. It seemed amazingly symmetrical, as though the work of well-trained circus birds. The supervisor smiled. This was the kind of exceptional moment he was missing because he no longer visited bridges. He would have to go back to doing so.

There was no chance to enjoy the gulls' unexpected show any longer because the rumbling of a truck suddenly came from the end of the bridge.

He didn't have to explain a thing. As soon as he'd been promoted to supervisor, he'd introduced military discipline. The District Administration was indeed a civilian service but there was a reason for the uniforms they wore. He gave a brief order and in no time at all ladders were placed on either side of the painting. He watched with satisfaction as the workers nimbly climbed up in unison as though they'd trained for just such an event. It was a shame that his excess weight had prevented him from becoming a military officer, as he'd wanted when he was young. He had a talent for command.

As the workers took positions on the railing around the painting, the supervisor heard murmurs behind him. He turned around and saw a group of five or six people on the other side of the bridge, standing there in lively conversation, watching the unusual sight. Wrapped up in gazing at the river, he hadn't heard them gather. Wasn't it early for so many people to be on the bridge? He looked at his wristwatch: it wasn't even seven. What he wanted was to order them to leave, but he lacked the appropriate authority. All he could do was sharply order the workers to hurry.

It would have been better without eyewitnesses, but if they quickly removed the canvas everything could still be kept secret. Rumors might spread, but if the police took note and came to investigate, he could show them the largest reproduction he had instead of the painting. They would have no reason to suspect he'd deluded them. It wasn't likely that anyone present would recognize the Yellow Bridge, particularly not shown from above. People usually made no distinction between bridges. They were all more or less the same to them.

The workers' agitation was the first sign that something was wrong. They were looking at the back of the painting, talking in low voices, shrugging their shoulders as they did their best. Finally the foreman said contritely:

"It can't be taken off."

"What do you mean, can't?" said the supervisor, almost shouting.

"It's not hung but attached."

"What do you mean, attached?" He lowered his voice, remembering that there were curious ears nearby. Before the foreman could reply, he motioned to him to come down.

"The canvas is stretched over a wooden frame and the frame seems to be glued to the metal. . . ." The foreman said this in a hushed voice, even though no one would have heard him from the other side of the bridge even if he'd spoken normally.

"So detach it." The supervisor also spoke in an unnecessary whisper that did not diminish his vexation.

"We can't. We tried to pry it off, even with a crowbar, but it didn't work."

"Good-for-nothings," hissed the supervisor.

"We can try with acid. Or fire."

"Under no circumstances! You are not to damage the canvas by any means! Is that understood?"

The foreman quickly nodded. "Yes."

"Now go back up there. And get your act together. If you can't get the better of a little glued wood, you don't deserve the position you hold. It will be easy to find a more skillful foreman than you."

The man practically flew up the ladder. Since he was short and stout, this had a comical effect. The supervisor smiled and then turned around with a frown. Now there were a dozen people gathered on the other side of the bridge and more were coming from both ends. In addition, a car had slowed down completely and the driver was staring upward inquisitively.

These aren't just passers-by, concluded the supervisor. Someone must have seen the painting before he got there. He'd forgotten to ask the guard about it. The news seemed to be spreading fast. If these bungling oafs on the railing didn't do something quickly, everything was ruined. This many people on the bridge would inevitably attract the police. Someone might already have reported that something was up. There were stool pigeons all over the place.

He raised his head by the railing and shouted, "Faster!"

Just as he said it, a large drop hit him in the middle of the forehead. He looked up worriedly even higher, toward the sky. The dawn had brought a clear morning, but it wouldn't stay that way for long. Gray clouds were rolling in from the southwest. This had escaped his notice because he'd been turned primarily towards the sunny east where the sky was still clear. And when he'd turned toward the spectators, the clouds hadn't seemed that close to the bridge.

"Faster," he repeated more briskly, but realized at once that hurrying them would do no good. Even though the workers were trying as hard as they could, the frame was still firmly attached to the railing. They might be able to detach it before the police arrived, but it could start raining at any moment and that would be a catastrophe. Something had to be done right away to protect the canvas.

"Four of you come down! Now!" shouted the supervisor.

The workers looked at each other briefly and then the foreman signaled to three of them to join him. As they rushed down the ladder, the supervisor gave a new order.

"Take the tarpaulin off the truck and cover the painting!"

Just three and a half minutes later a dark purple tarpaulin covered the canvas. The supervisor breathed a sigh of relief. This had turned out better than he'd expected. The painting was not only safe, it could not be seen. If the police were to come, they wouldn't know which painting was under the tarpaulin and that was certainly propitious. . . .

"Carry on, carry on!" said the supervisor, seeing that the workers on the railing were waiting to receive further orders.

Drops splattered on the pavement, falling faster and faster. The group of bystanders who now numbered two dozen grew agitated. Several umbrellas were opened and two or three of them ran to the ends of the bridge. As though following an unspoken order, the workers pulled on their hoods at the same time.

The supervisor looked toward the guardhouse. There was no need to shout. The guard was already running toward him, opening an umbrella along the way, and the driver had just gotten into the car. They reached the middle at the same time. The supervisor stood there for a moment, undecided, and then looked at the sky again. Just as he stepped toward the open door of the car parked in front of the truck, the wailing of a police siren came from the other end of the bridge. He sighed and remained standing by the curb. The guard approached and raised the umbrella over him, and the driver closed the back door and returned to his seat.

∽ 5 ∾

THE POLICE CAR DREW up facing the official car from the District Bridge Administration. The inspector turned off the engine and got out. He was wearing a long ash-colored raincoat and dark wide-brimmed hat. Bony and tall, with a haggard face and thick mustache, he stared at the spectacle on the bridge railing.

The workers stopped what they were doing. In their dark purple capes, they seemed to have fused with the rectangle of the same color.

Before approaching the supervisor, the inspector eyed the people on the upstream side.

"Good morning," he said with a smile, looking downstream. "Interesting day."

"Interesting," agreed the supervisor, returning his smile.

"Rain and sun at the same time. You don't see that very often."

The supervisor's smile broadened. "You really don't."

"Maybe there'll be a rainbow."

"It could easily happen."

"Rainbow days are interesting. It's like something unusual always happens. Have you noticed? But of course it's just a coincidence. Strange things also happen on days without a rainbow. Even so, it makes you wonder . . . Well, all right, never mind." He motioned with his head toward the railing. "Is something interesting happening here too? I see you've got a crowd."

"Nothing special. We're taking something down. Curious people are drawn to all sorts of things. We'll be done in no time at all." The supervisor clapped his plump hands twice. "Get to work!"

The capes snapped out of their stiff positions.

"Interesting," noted the inspector. "And might I know what you're taking down?"

"Just a painting."

"A painting? Very interesting. It's this big?" He spread his arms.

"Yes."

"Extraordinarily interesting. Do you know how long it takes to paint a large painting? One, for example, of this size? Up to a year. A painter told me that. Even though he worked quite industriously, his opus was very modest. Barely thirty paintings for all his years as an artist. He'd have been much more productive if he'd painted small canvases. But that, it seems, was beneath his dignity. Artists are a vain lot."

"As soon as we finish the people will disperse. And the rain will chase them away. There are fewer of them already."

A dozen bystanders remained, pressed under four umbrellas. Another three or four had only caps or hoods for protection. The rain had gotten stronger in the meantime. A car passed without stopping.

"What's a painting doing on the railing? But why am I asking? Of course! The District Bridge Administration put it up. Congratulations. It's a credit to you for being the first. Public services otherwise have no affinity for the arts, which is a shame. Why shouldn't exhibits be organized on bridges, I ask you? When it's not raining, of course. Is there any more open and well-lighted display space? Or theater productions in the sewers? Most plays don't require any scenery. The best place to give concerts is in prisons. Have you ever been in prison?"

The supervisor briskly shook his head without speaking.

"Interesting. Never?"

"Never."

"You're missing a lot. The acoustics are extraordinary. Only bare walls. You should go sometime. I can help if you want."

"I'd love to, but I'm awfully busy. . . ."

"In any case, let me congratulate you once more on this move. Truly extraordinary. Although a bit more cooperation among public services wouldn't hurt.

It's always a good idea to cooperate with the police. If you'd told us you were putting up an exhibit here, we could have given you a hand. There wouldn't be a crowd." He pointed his thumb over his shoulder to the opposite side. "We know how to deal with people."

"We didn't expect a crowd. . . ."

"Interesting. You organize an exhibit and don't expect anyone to turn up. And when they do, you take down the painting. That's not because of the rain. I see it's well protected. So what's going on?"

The supervisor glanced at the guard who was holding the umbrella stiffly. He hadn't raised his hood and rain was pouring down his bowed head.

"What's going on . . . uh, you see . . . this isn't an exhibit."

"Extremely interesting. It isn't an exhibit but there is a painting. And what would a painting be doing on a bridge if there isn't an exhibit?"

"It was put up during the night."

"More and more interesting. And who put it there?"

The supervisor shrugged his shoulders. "We don't know."

"You don't know? Don't you have a guard on the bridge?"

"We do." The supervisor motioned with his chin toward the man with the umbrella. "But he fell asleep."

The guard raised his head, disconcerted, but the scowl he received in return forced him to lower it again.

The inspector looked at the guard as though he'd just become aware of his presence.

"Your staff aren't very reliable. If a policeman had fallen asleep on the job, he would have lost it."

"He will be punished. We have strict regulations too. But this has never happened to him before."

"One more interesting thing. The first time the guard falls asleep on duty is when someone decides to put a painting on the bridge. Well, all right. Let's say that's what happened. So why wasn't the incident reported to us instead of us having to hear about it . . . second-hand? You realize this is clearly a case for the police."

"We didn't want to bother you needlessly. It's nothing . . . serious. Just an ordinary daub by some eccentric. They often leave things on the bridge. Should we call you every time? We'll remove it at once." He looked at the workers. "Is it ready?"

The foreman spread his arms helplessly and the supervisor gave the inspector an awkward smile.

"It's glued on rather hard. But we'll take care of it in no time. . . ."

"What's on that . . . daub . . . that's so big?"

"Nothing worth mentioning. Just a bridge. . . ."

"Here's something else that's interesting. A bridge on a bridge. That's an inspector's mind for you, noticing such a coincidence. It usually leads nowhere, but now and again it can be useful. I'd really like to see the painting."

"The rain would ruin it if we took off the tarpaulin. You can drop by the District Bridge Administration later."

"What's the shame in ruining a daub?"

The supervisor motioned his head briefly to the other side of the bridge.

"It wouldn't leave a nice impression. . . ."

"Oh, yes. If the police were here and no one else, then it would be all right. But why should two public services be accused of barbaric behavior? How about just lifting the tarpaulin a little, so I can get a peek? I hope you don't mind my curiosity."

The supervisor quickly tried to think of a reason not to comply, but nothing occurred to him. He gave the order grudgingly. Pulling the rope along the edge of the tarpaulin, the workers raised it. The inspector and the supervisor stood under the slanted shelter thus formed. The guard came up too, still holding the umbrella over his superior's head, although this was no longer necessary.

If the inspector hadn't been staring at the painting, he might have seen the supervisor's dumbfounded expression. And the guard's even more dumbfounded expression that the supervisor failed to see as well. They spent a minute and a half under the shelter in silence, then all three went back into the rain and the tarpaulin was lowered.

"Interesting . . . daub," said the inspector, the first to speak.

"You were right," said the supervisor, his voice somewhat quieter than usual. "This is a job for the police, not the District Bridge Administration. I wanted to help, but I don't have the people for it. You can see for yourself. My guards sleep on the job and my workers can't even detach an ordinary painting. They've been fooling around with it for half an hour already."

Gesturing sharply without speaking, he ordered the foreman to get his men off the railing. Dark purple capes quickly slid down the ladders.

"It's good when public services know how responsibility is distributed," replied the inspector. "Don't worry, this is now safely in the hands of the police. Feel free to bother us whenever something like this turns up. We've got people who are awake and also people skilled at detaching things."

The supervisor nodded his head with a forced smile,

then turned to the workers. With a new sharp move of his hand he sent them to the truck bed. They would go back to the District Bridge Administration building without the tarpaulin. As punishment. Then he went up to his car, waited for the driver to open the door and settled on the back seat with his usual difficulty.

The guard headed back to the guardhouse bareheaded in the downpour. He was so bewildered that he kept on carrying the umbrella in front of him, still not thinking to raise his hood. The only thing he managed to conclude was that his superior was right. The best thing would be to take early retirement. The bridge wasn't the place for him anymore.

When the car took off in front of the truck, there was room for only one thought in the supervisor's head too. He highly valued original paintings. But not quite that original.

∽ 6 ∾

WHEN HE WAS ALONE on the downstream side of the bridge, the inspector turned to look upstream. There was no need to do or say anything. He just stared at the crowd over the roof of the police car as rain poured off his hat brim. Less than two minutes later there was no one facing him. He went around the car, sat behind the wheel and put his hat on the passenger seat, unconcerned that he would get the upholstery wet.

It's no wonder, he thought with a smile, that everything's wrong in the District Bridge Administration, with such a block-headed and inept supervisor. Indeed, only a dull-witted person would claim this painting was a daub. But this was a stroke of luck. Had the supervisor been more knowledgeable about art, he would have understood what was within reach, and had he known how to handle his subordinates, the painting would have been taken off the railing before the police were informed that something unusual was happening on the Black Bridge. And then most likely all trace of the painting would have disappeared.

The inspector's smile broadened. It was actually a double stroke of luck. If he hadn't replaced a colleague, he wouldn't have been on duty. And that colleague would have seen just a daub under the tarpaulin too. Police inspectors knew as much about art as the District Bridge Administration's supervisor. He himself would have been no exception if it hadn't been for the case of a well-known art forger he'd handled about a year ago. The job had forced him to delve into the matter more deeply.

He had mentioned the man to the supervisor—the painter only interested in large paintings—without actually revealing what he did. His copies were so faithful that only the greatest experts could distinguish them from the originals. The investigation had lasted a long time because evidence was hard to find. When he finally got his hands on it, he hadn't turned the case over to the prosecutor, but covered it up instead.

He'd been amply rewarded for his benevolence. An enormous painting covered one of the walls in the basement of a small house in the country where he never took anyone. He went there whenever he had a weekend free and sat in front of it for a long time. At first he'd intended to sell it—during the investigation he'd discovered that there was a very profitable black market for high-quality copies—but the longer he looked at it the harder it was to part with. It was so beautiful that he could almost overlook the fact that it was a forgery.

And now he suddenly had a chance to get hold of the original. That was the first thing that occurred to him when he glanced at the painting under the tarpaulin and recognized the original of his copy from the basement. Even a much more minor coincidence than this should have aroused his suspicions, but his natural mistrust was completely suppressed by the desire to capitalize on this unique opportunity.

He'd been an inspector for a long time and knew how to control his emotions, so no astonishment had shown on his face. It had been expressionless, like an experienced poker player's. In any case, even if his jaw had dropped in amazement, that ninny of a fat supervisor wouldn't have noticed a thing.

If it hadn't been this very painting, he would naturally have wondered how it got there. But now it made no difference. Most likely a fanatical art lover had stolen it—although the inspector had yet to receive a report of a theft—and put it here for some reason or other. What else could be the case? Indeed, it would have made more sense to take it to the place it depicted, the Red Bridge in Bratislava, but who knew what made madmen tick? In that event it would have been out of his reach.

Had the painting been smaller, he could have done everything by himself. He would have taken it off the railing, put it in his car, driven to his country house, put it in place of the copy, and handed the copy over to police storage. Only a little over an hour would be needed. After the painting was returned to its owner, the fact that it was a fake might be discovered when checking whether it had been damaged, but the thief would be blamed for the switch. Only the forger would have reason to suspect the inspector, but no danger threatened from that quarter.

But since the canvas was too big, he would have to try something else. He would call the technical unit to take the painting down and move it to his office. Then he would go to his country house, take the copy out of its frame, roll it up to make it as small as possible, and return to his office. He would make the switch there, then take the original to his country house and put it in the frame.

A smile spread over the inspector's face again. Luck was still on his side. Today was Sunday so the police station would be almost empty. Everything would be done quite inconspicuously.

He could radio the technical unit right away. They weren't the bungling workers of the District Bridge Administration but professionals skilled at much more complex jobs than taking paintings off railings. The canvas would be down in no time flat. He decided to wait a bit, however. The sky seemed to be opening up. He couldn't see the end of the bridge from the downpour. Although the tarpaulin was properly protecting the painting, something might go wrong when it was being taken down and there was no reason to hurry.

But there would have been reason to hurry without the rain. Too many people had seen the painting and someone among them must work for State Security. They had no fewer informers than the police. They must have already received word that something unusual was happening on the bridge. Stolen paintings were not State Security's jurisdiction but some wise guy there might come and check things out anyway. They were notorious for sticking their nose where it didn't belong. This would not necessarily spoil the inspector's plan, but everything would be more difficult and entangled. The best thing was not to have State Security on your back. Not only in special situations like this but in general.

They were unlikely to go out in such a downpour and would probably bide their time until the bad weather passed. They were indeed overly curious and eager, but after all, not that much. Particularly since they knew the police were already on the scene. And it was Sunday morning.

The smartest thing would be to call the technical unit right away. By the time they got there, the rain might have eased off. They could pre-empt State Security. Just as he reached for the radio, something started drumming on the roof of the car. The inspector first thought it was hail. He wondered anxiously whether the tarpaulin offered sufficient protection. It seemed sturdy enough, but you never knew with hail.

Panic was already getting the upper hand when his experienced inspector's eye noted something that didn't add up. Even though drumming continued on the roof, neither the windshield nor the hood had any trace of icy balls. Raindrops, now tapering off, were all he saw. He looked in the rear view mirror and saw no hail on the back window either.

He picked up his hat from the seat next to him and put it on, then cautiously got out of the car. As soon as he was outside, a shrieking was heard from somewhere up above that overpowered the sound of the rain. For some reason he hadn't heard it when he was inside. He didn't look up, though, because his eyes were riveted on the car right in front of him. Never in his life had he seen such a fouled car roof. Bending his head back slowly, he stared at a flock of a dozen river gulls. They were circling at a low altitude, making unbearable noise and dropping mushy bombs exclusively on the middle part of the car. Just as he was wondering how they could be so precise, the next bomb missed the target and hit him partially on the rim of his hat and partially on his forehead.

He quickly withdrew to the shelter of the car. Just as he closed the door behind him, the drumming on the roof stopped. As he wiped his forehead and then his hat with a handkerchief, he tried to make sense out of the unusual incident, but all he managed to conclude was that something fishy was going on. The sooner he left the bridge the better. He reached for his radio again but was interrupted once more. When someone knocked on the passenger window, he almost jumped out of his seat.

∽ 7 ∾

HE STARED OUT OF the window, eyes wide open, but what he saw was completely harmless. An elderly man was smiling at him from the other side of the glass. He had a pleasant face, thick gray hair and sported a red bow tie. He was rather short so he didn't have to bend down very far. In one hand was an umbrella and in the other was a little white poodle.

The inspector wondered how he'd missed him a moment before. Sure, he'd been preoccupied with the car roof and gulls, but he certainly should have noticed that someone was coming his way. And on the same side of the bridge. He was proud of his eye for detail, as befits an inspector, and here he'd missed an entire man. Not very large, but nevertheless . . . Those damned birds must have really rattled him.

Be that as it may, he didn't have time for idle citizens right now. And a slightly crazy one, it would seem. Would any normal person take a poodle for a walk in a storm? He frowned, his mouth already open to snap out something, when the old man shifted the little dog to the hand with the umbrella and plunged his free hand into the pocket of his white raincoat. He took something out and pressed it against the window.

The inspector swallowed the lump in his throat, recognizing the badge of State Security. He had underestimated them several times over. Indeed, should rain on a Sunday morning decrease the service's vigilance? And then the little old man. Even though the inspector was trained to be distrustful, the man with the poodle was the last person he would have suspected of being an agent. Finally, his mysterious materialization was now explained. The inspector had to hand it to them. They were really skilled at keeping a low profile.

He quickly reached across and opened the door. The old man had already bent down to get into the car and then noticed the puddle on the passenger seat. He didn't say anything. He just straightened up and moved to the back door. First the inspector tried to reach the handle from where he was sitting, but this didn't work. He thought briefly of kneeling on the seat and trying from there, but realized it would be simpler to get out. He went around the back of the car, opened one door and closed the other. As he went around the front of the car to the driver's seat, he looked up for a moment. The rain was now just a drizzle and not a river gull was in sight.

"You car's not very clean," said the old man, speaking first. Although this was a reproach, his voice sounded cordial. He put the poodle down next to him and laid the umbrella at his feet. "Wet seat, terrible dirty roof that not even the downpour washed off . . . Such untidiness does not befit a police officer."

"Circumstances, . . ." mumbled the inspector, turning halfway toward the agent.

"I hope the circumstances didn't prevent you from investigating the case. What have you established?"

"Not much yet, but . . ."

"Let's hear what little you have."

"Someone put up a painting here during the night. People from the District Bridge Administration got here before me and tried to take it down, but they were unsuccessful. They were rather inept. But at least they covered it with a tarpaulin."

The old man waited a moment, petting the dog.

"Is that it?"

"For now. As soon as the rain stops. . . ."

"The rain has probably washed away the traces, if there were any. And something could have been done while it was raining. Did you question the guard, for example?"

"There was no need. He doesn't know anything. Instead of keeping watch over the bridge, he was sleeping."

"Who told you that?"

"The District Bridge Administration supervisor."

"So, secondhand. It's always better to rely on firsthand information. The guard swore to us that he didn't sleep a wink."

When did they find time to question him, wondered the inspector. Barely ten minutes had passed since he'd gone back to the guardhouse. They must have gone in when the downpour was strongest, when he couldn't see the end of the bridge.

"He's lying. He's afraid of losing his job. If he was

awake, why didn't he see anything? You couldn't slip a painting as big as this to the top of the bridge."

"Who knows? What if he's telling the truth? Maybe he really didn't see anything on the bridge."

"So how did the painting get there?"

The old man smiled and petted the poodle again.

"Isn't it obvious?"

"I'm afraid not," replied the inspector after a moment's consideration.

"One would expect someone with a job like yours to have more imagination."

The inspector's voice was tinged with embarrassment. "I really don't see how . . ."

"From above or below. There's no third possibility."

"You mean . . . ?"

"The painting could have been brought by a quiet craft to the base of the bridge. A sailboat, let's say. Those who put it in place climbed up from the outer side of the railing."

"That would be some feat."

"I agree. It would be even harder to do it from above."

"By helicopter?"

"Certainly not. They make a terrible noise. Even if the guard was sleeping, he would have been wakened for sure. And so would people who live near the bridge. The aircraft had to be soundless."

The inspector's eyes started to dance before he spoke. "A balloon!"

"In all probability. Or a dirigible, but they are harder to come by."

The brief silence that settled was broken by the poodle letting out something like a belch.

"Sorry. She's been suffering from indigestion for some time. The rigors of old age."

The inspector stared at the white dog for a few moments.

"It still seems more probable to me that the guard was sleeping."

"If you had my experience, you'd know that the simplest explanation is not necessarily the most probable. Occam is not always right."

"Who?"

"Never mind."

"But why would someone embark on such a complicated and risky enterprise just to put a painting on the bridge?"

"That is the question we need to answer. The solution to the mystery might lie hidden in the painting itself. Let's see what we know about it. Did you, for example, determine its exact measurements? That can be done over the tarpaulin."

"There was no chance. And why would that be important?"

"You never know what might be important. We measured it from the outside. Just in case. The painting is 243 centimeters wide and 171 high."

The inspector was briefly tempted to ask when they'd measured it, but refrained. It was unlikely he would get an answer.

"Interesting."

"Yes. Paintings with those dimensions are rare. But let's put aside technical details for a moment. You saw the painting, didn't you?"

"Not very well. The workers raised the tarpaulin a little. It was rather dark underneath it."

"But you did see something."

"Yes, but the supervisor could tell you more. He saw the painting before it was covered by the tarpaulin."

"Right now what you have to say is more interesting. You know a thing or two about art, don't you?"

The inspector scrutinized the old man's cheerful face for a moment before answering.

"Very little."

"You are too modest. You certainly must have acquired considerable knowledge for an inspector when you conducted the case of the famous paintings that were forged. It's a shame the case wasn't closed, although I'm sure you gave it your best."

The poodle belched again. The agent reached into an inside pocket, took out a handkerchief the same color as his bow tie and wiped the dog around her muzzle.

"Don't hold it against her. She's having a hard time." He put the handkerchief back in his pocket. "So, what can you tell us about the canvas? Did you recognize it perhaps?"

The inspector shook his head slowly.

"Are you sure?"

"I'm sure."

The old man looked at his collocutor intently for a few moments, then reached for the outside pocket of his raincoat. He took out a photograph and passed it between the front seats.

"Could this be the painting under the tarpaulin?"

The familiar sight of the Red Bridge in Bratislava did not upset the inspector as much as what surrounded it. Like a thin frame, the chestnut paneling on the basement wall of his country house could be seen around the edge of the photograph.

"I wouldn't know . . . It was hard to see under the tarpaulin."

He realized there was no sense in dragging things out. He'd been exposed. Whenever he caught a criminal, what irritated him most was for them to keep on claiming their innocence even after being presented with the evidence against them. That's how he was acting now. He'd already opened his mouth to confess, but the agent spoke first.

"We'll clear this up immediately." He pointed out of the window. "It seems the rain has stopped."

He picked up the poodle and umbrella, opened the door and got out of the car, then bent down and looked inside.

"After you," he said with a broad smile.

When the inspector got out in front of the car, he saw four men in gray overalls under the painting. They were holding long boat-hooks. He could have sworn they hadn't been there a moment before. He looked around the wet bridge. Everything was deserted.

He went around the car and joined the old man who was standing by the curb. The boat-hooks arched upward, caught the rope and raised the tarpaulin.

Although the painting was still in shadow, one look was enough. The old man turned toward the inspector where confusion and relief were fighting for priority on his face.

"I won't keep you any longer. It was nice to make your acquaintance."

The inspector mumbled something unintelligible, then headed for the other side of the car. He was just about to settle into the seat when the agent's voice stopped him.

"Have a good time in the country." He picked up the little dog. "We all have a right to our hobbies."

8

THE OLD MAN WAS not normally inclined to forgive sins. In any other situation he would have let the inspector go, making it quite clear that he had him over a barrel and expected services. Now, however, he'd revealed that they were on to his secret and offered him the chance to get rid of the evidence in the basement of his country house. But it made no difference. Even if he destroyed the copy, the awareness that State Security had their eyes on him would leave its mark. Not much persuasion would be necessary if they needed him. He would never know for sure what else they had on him, and no one has just one sin. Particularly not a police inspector.

He'd sent him away as soon as possible because he didn't want any witnesses. What he'd seen under the tarpaulin required the utmost secrecy. Unfortunately, the painting had been seen by considerably more eyes than were desirable. He wasn't very worried about those he'd found next to it—employees of the District Bridge Administration and the police. Employees of public services were notorious for their poor powers of observation. Whoever said that two people can look at the exact same thing and see something different must have had them in mind.

He was most uncomfortable with the alleged random onlookers on the other side of the bridge. State Security informers had been there, but there might have been others too. The world was teeming with various agents. He of all people knew that. News about the mysterious incident on the Black Bridge in Regensburg had spread very far. A state of emergency had been declared in intelligence circles around the world when the most sought-after work of art of their profession—a painting of Budapest's White Bridge—had turned up out of nowhere.

Someone uninformed would never understand why the seemingly ordinary painting of an old bridge at dusk had caused so much excitement in the top echelons of the intelligence services. Well, not exactly ordinary, it was clearly a valuable work of art, but this was hardly crucial. In the world of intelligence agents, artistic merits have never been particularly esteemed.

But the merits of concealing are. The innocent scene of the bridge was just a front. Inaccessible to the naked eye, underneath it was hidden something coveted by various secret services. Although the painter was talented and had gained renown as an artist, he'd enjoyed even greater respect—although not publicly—as an intelligence agent. One day when he was suddenly found dead, it turned out he'd been a fourfold agent.

Everything he left behind had been searched with a fine-toothed comb, but nothing was found that would compromise the four sides he worked for. Everyone was relieved, but not for long. During preparations for a retrospective exhibit in a gallery, ultraviolet lighting accidentally revealed extensive writing under the layer of paint on the picture of Budapest's White Bridge. The police were informed but when they arrived they found the gallery owner dead. Not a trace was left of the large painting.

The person who'd taken it came into possession of valuable data. Everyone thought they would try to sell it—many were prepared to offer great sums for the information in order to safeguard their own secrets and get hold of others'—but nothing was put on offer. The earth seemed to have swallowed up the painting, which made no sense at all.

A bridge was probably the last place one would expect it to appear. The old man reproached himself for his poor intuition. That possibility should have come to mind when he received word that a painting had been found on the railing, particularly since there was no simple explanation as to how it got there. And he certainly should have guessed what it might be after they had measured it. He hadn't forgotten the dimensions of the painting that had disappeared, but he hadn't connected them to the size of this canvas. Indeed, the numbers were slightly different because this painting had been measured over the tarpaulin, but that was no excuse. It seemed the years were slowly catching up with him.

The little poodle in his arms raised its head to him. He smiled and petted it. It was time to provide for a suitable pension for the two of them. State Security amply rewarded their former employees, but he nevertheless considered it insufficient. This was a unique opportunity to provide himself with what he deserved for the rest of his life.

He couldn't keep the painting, but fortunately this was not necessary. It would be enough to be close by when the painting was exposed to ultraviolet light. His photographic memory would do the rest and no one would be any the wiser.

He turned his head toward his left shoulder and spoke into the button on the edge of his shoulder strap. Just as he finished, a van headed from the guardhouse toward the middle of the bridge. The signs on the side panels indicated it belonged to a company that serviced air conditioners. The van stopped under the painting. Four men in overalls opened the rear door, put away the boat-hooks and took out two extension ladders and a toolbox. Two men climbed up either side of the painting. Not a word was spoken.

The attack started when a power saw was heading for one of the places where the wooden frame with the stretched canvas was glued to the railing. It was so sudden that the man dropped his tool and almost fell. At first he wasn't sure what had swooped down on him, and then gulls pounced on the other three men.

Just like kamikazes, they dived on them in waves. Although there were only a dozen of them, it seemed like a lot more. The impact of their beaks was painful, so that the silence of the bridge was torn by yowls of pain. It took a good two minutes before one of the men being attacked came to his senses and pulled out his revolver. But before he fired it, a short order came from the ground in an old man's voice.

Instead of retaliating, the four men quickly climbed down the ladders. The gulls did not continue their attack. They soared up toward the sky and started circling above the bridge. Looking up, the agent caressed the little dog and whispered something in its ear to calm it. When he was certain the danger had passed, he turned toward his subordinates to give them instructions, but before he could speak a vehicle was heard from the other end of the bridge.

At the sight of an open jeep on its way toward him, the old man sighed.

"I should have known," he mumbled to whomever was listening through the microphone in the button. "This certainly couldn't happen without them."

9

A GIRL WITH LONG blond hair under her helmet stood up in the passenger seat when the jeep stopped next to the van in the middle of the bridge. She was extremely tall, so standing in the vehicle she seemed gigantic. The sleeves of her camouflage uniform were rolled up to the elbow and there was a short swagger stick under her left arm. With a broad smile, she jumped elegantly onto the pavement under the painting.

"You organize a party but don't invite the ladies," she said to the old man, ostensibly in reproof. "I might even think this is a men-only get-together." She wagged her finger at him coquettishly.

The agent did not reply. He tried to keep his face expressionless, but the twitching of tiny wrinkles around his eyes betrayed his displeasure.

The girl drew close and stretched out her hand to the poodle. She didn't remove it when the little dog growled softly and scratched it behind the ear.

"Still plagued by indigestion? Did you try mint tea? Poor Fifi."

"It's not Fifi," said the old man through clenched teeth. "How many times do I have to tell you?"

"You shouldn't take it with you everywhere. Dogs are much more sensitive than humans. When they see that something shady is going on, they react psychosomatically. And just about everything around you is shady. That's the profession you're in."

"Yours isn't any better. But there's nothing here for Military Security. This is our case."

The girl raised her eyes to the sky where there were no longer any birds.

"You don't seem to be handling it very well."

"We'd already be finished if you weren't wasting my time."

"I thought you liked my company. But I won't keep you. I just want to peer under the tarpaulin. I'm an art lover too."

"You don't say. That must be something new. As of this morning, for example."

"Oh, no. I've been interested in a particular style for some time. Naiveism."

"Naiveism?"

"Yes. You haven't heard of it? That's strange. The style is a favorite among naive State Security agents."

"Who's naive?" The old man raised his voice for the first time on the bridge.

"An agent who believes that a painting everyone is after will appear out of nowhere within his reach. And that it's the original untouched painting. Particularly unchanged in the deeper layer that can only be seen under special lighting."

The old man stared at the girl through narrowed eyes. He wanted to respond in kind but nothing suitable came to mind. A few moments passed in tense silence and then she turned toward the men in overalls.

"Raise the tarpaulin."

First they looked at each other and then all eyes turned to the agent. Silence reigned once again.

The girl took the swagger stick from under her arm and struck her right thigh.

"Well?"

The old man sighed and then nodded his head.

With swift movements, the ladders and toolbox were put back in the van and the boat-hooks were taken out. Another shelter was raised above the canvas.

The girl was so completely engrossed in the painting

that she missed the barely perceptible spasm that flitted over the old man's face.

"I'd say you were right," he said in a conciliatory voice. "We really didn't handle it well. I wish you better luck."

He snapped his fingers and pointed to the van. First the boat-hooks were put in the back of the van and then the four men got inside. The old man sat down next to the driver.

Once they had left, he started stroking the poodle's back. Actually, when he gave it more thought, they didn't need any extra income. A State Security agent's pension was more than enough for their modest needs.

~ 10 ~

IT REALLY WAS TIME for the State Security agent to retire, thought the girl wistfully after being left alone on the bridge with the driver who had brought her in the jeep. Although she often needled the old man, she actually found him sweet with that little dog that never left his side. In his younger days he had been considered a great master of his trade and lectures were given about his exploits in intelligence schools, but we all have a life expectancy and his had clearly expired. He'd have done better to bow out than ruin his reputation with incredible blunders.

He hadn't even recognized the painting under the tarpaulin. It wasn't Budapest's White Bridge as he'd reported to headquarters. His eyesight must have deteriorated and he didn't want to admit it so he didn't wear glasses. And of course the case wasn't theirs. Fortunately, he'd been sensible enough to understand that in the end.

The painting of Novi Sad's Blue Bridge was clearly a matter for Military Security. This was a message from their opponents that they were on to their deepest secret. They were flouting their superiority, arrogantly humiliating them, having spared no effort to get hold of the famous painting and bring it secretly all the way here, just to show that they knew about operation "Blue Bridge." That they had their people at the very top. Heads would roll for this, not only in the military intelligence service but at headquarters as well.

She looked up at the sky that had partially cleared in the meantime. The storm had headed north. Only someone who knew what they were looking for would have seen a bright spot in the blue space between two clouds.

"You've seen the painting," said the girl softly, barely moving her lips. "What do you want us to do?"

The bug in her left ear did not reply at once. The girl kept looking up, blinking.

"Well?" she repeated impatiently.

"Destroy it," came a rasping male voice.

"Excuse me?" She wasn't one to doubt, but now she couldn't help herself.

"The order came from upstairs."

"But why? What a shame, it's such a pretty picture. We can take it down." She stopped, then added with a smile, "I'd be happy to keep it if no one needs it."

"Very funny. You know they're watching us. We have to pay them back properly. A scorching message is the only thing they'll understand. Flamethrowers will be on the bridge any moment."

Less than a minute later, a second jeep was parked behind the first one. Three soldiers jumped out of it with metal cylinders on their backs and visors lowered over their faces. They were holding long hoses with bluish flames already undulating at the nozzles.

"Move back a little," said one of the soldiers to the girl as they raised their flame throwers.

Not wanting to watch, the girl lowered her eyes. So she missed the beginning of the last act of the gulls' show.

They flew under the bridge without being heard. Like a perfectly trained airborne unit, the dozen birds spread out on the upper edge of the covered painting. Plunging their beaks into the tarpaulin, they flew off just a moment before the fiery tongues gushed upward from the bridge's pavement.

Fire engulfed the iron frame of the railing, but not the painting that was supposed to be there.

"Stop!" shouted the girl, but this was unnecessary since the flamethrowers had already turned off their equipment. With their smoking hoses lowered, the soldiers along with the girl and two drivers stared at the soaring flock as it carried the tarpaulin and what was underneath it.

When the birds dropped their load in unison and flew away in all directions, they realized that nothing was there.

As the tarpaulin fell, the effects of aerodynamics opened it up. This slowed it down as it descended, swaying gently left and right like a leaf falling from a branch. It touched the Danube's water like a large dark purple cover, rested on the surface briefly as though hesitating what to do next, then sank. The river drew it in, leaving not a trace behind.

The six observers by the railing stared at the spot where it had disappeared a little while longer, as though expecting it to resurface.

The girl was the first to snap out of it.

"Well?" she said quietly, raising her eyes.

No answer came from the bright spot in the sky.

"Well?" she repeated in a louder voice a few moments later.

"Return to base," said the rasping male voice.

"What about the painting?"

"What painting?"

Second Wonder
Yellow Bridge, Vienna

ON SUNDAY, AT 23:49, something happened on the
Yellow Bridge in Vienna.

Not a single tram was crossing the Danube at that
hour. There were only five people on the bridge. Two
were going toward the left bank and three toward the
right, looking downstream. Four were on foot and one
was riding a bicycle.

They all suddenly stopped without knowing why.
They simply stopped in mid-step and the cyclist braked
and put his foot on the pavement. Being some distance
apart, none of them noticed that the same thing was
happening to the others.

The standstill lasted barely two or three seconds. An
onlooker—a passenger on the deck of a boat approaching the bridge, for example, or a voyeur on an upper
floor of one of the nearby skyscrapers examining the
area around the river with binoculars—might have
thought, even though it was unlikely, that they had
all suddenly remembered something that made them
change the direction in which they were going. But
there was no such onlooker and the conclusion would

be wrong, because when they soon continued, none of them changed direction.

Although this seemed to be an innocuous event, the five people wondered what had happened. This was inevitable, of course. And something different crossed each one's mind.

~ 2 ~

THAT'S THE SHADOW OF DEATH, thought the theater prompter.

She was otherwise a cheerful woman, still of an age where death rarely, if ever, crossed her mind. And death would have been unlikely to creep into her thoughts if the play that evening hadn't revolved around it. She greatly preferred comedies, but prompters don't compile theater repertoires.

Not only had there been a tragedy on the program, but an incident near the end had almost jeopardized the performance. The elderly principal actor was suddenly taken ill. The audience failed to notice because his role required him to have a heart attack right then. He seemed to be giving a striking performance. There was even a round of applause.

The prompter alone suspected that he wasn't acting. He collapsed next to her box. His forehead was beaded with sweat, the corners of his mouth were foaming and his breathing was irregular. He looked at her with wide-open eyes and seemed to be telling her by sign language that he truly wasn't well.

She was filled with panic and didn't know what to do. She couldn't leave her post to tell someone backstage. The other three actors continued as though everything was fine, clearly unaware of the problem. If she raised the alarm, commotion would ensue and the play would be in jeopardy.

And the play could not be interrupted, of course. Not at any price. That was the hallowed rule of the theater. Furthermore, she would be the cause of a scandal. Particularly if it turned out that she was mistaken and it had been excellent acting.

She decided to pretend she hadn't noticed. No one could hold that against her. The others hadn't detected anything unusual either. If anyone reproached her, she had a credible excuse. She was engrossed in her job—carefully following the text of the play.

Besides, everything might still turn out fine. The play would shortly end and the actor had no other lines. All he had to do was lie there onstage and breathe his last. He received more applause for his convincing death.

When the curtain dropped and he stayed on the floor, everyone flocked around him. Fortunately he still gave signs of life. He was quickly taken offstage so the curtain could rise again. The audience had expected him to appear with his colleagues to receive a well-deserved final round of applause, but at that point they were putting him into an ambulance. The latest news from the hospital was that an operation was underway and the outcome was uncertain.

Waiting to find out more, the prompter and the entire troupe had stayed at the theater longer than usual. No one had asked her anything. Finally she had to leave to catch the last tram. When she got out of the theater, however, she decided to walk home.

As she'd hoped, the fresh air helped to chase away the somber thoughts. Her cheerful disposition was also a contributing factor. But as she was crossing the bridge, death suddenly crept up on her once again.

∽ 3 ∾

A SECOND BAD SIGN, thought the contract killer.

He was a superstitious man on the threshold of his seventh decade. He kept track of portentous signs before every assignment. He would pull out if there were more than two, even though this brought him nothing but trouble. Losing his high fee was not the worst of it. Those putting out the contract were unhappy with the outcome and had no understanding of his reasons. And these were not people to be dealt with lightly. One even sought the services of another contract killer to get even. But he'd outsmarted him.

He always thoroughly reconnoitered the area where the murder would take place. Extensive preparation was vital in his profession. Late that evening he'd spent some forty minutes on the small square opposite the house where the next day's victim lived. He'd sat unobtrusively on a bench and fed pigeons under the branches of a tall linden. There was no way anyone could guess why he'd visited the little park.

Just as he expected, the man he was supposed to kill appeared at the front door right on time with a Pekingese on a leash. He respected people who kept to a routine, as he did. They made his job much easier, unlike those without, where something was always likely to go wrong. With this assignment, everything should go smoothly.

Just as he thought this, something unexpected happened. The Pekingese suddenly ran across the street, attracted by something on the other side of the square. Although tiny, it tugged its surprised owner.

The man lost his balance, stumbled and fell flat on the pavement. There were no cars close by, but one could appear at any moment. Since it was a round-about, the driver would only spot someone lying on the road at the last instant.

The contract killer immediately recognized this as a bad sign, but he didn't hesitate. As the only eyewitness to the accident, he rushed to help the man up. It was a matter of professional pride. How could he let some amateur do his job, personified by a random driver?

He forced a smile at the man's gratitude and turned down the offer to drop by his house for a drink with the excuse that it was already late. They shook hands cordially when they parted and he even petted the little dog's head.

He headed for his hotel on foot even though it was rather far. He never took a taxi after reconnoitering. It was a precautionary measure; the fewer people the better to see and remember him near the scene of the next day's murder. The man with the Pekingese certainly hadn't forgotten him but this was not a worry. His memory would not be long-lived.

Walking slowly through the cool night, he thought about the incident on the small square. He had never met one of his victims before. A feeling of unease came over him regarding what lay ahead the next day. He'd never felt anything similar before. This was not because he was hardhearted; until now he had shot at faceless targets. This time the target had a face and a voice. Cordiality and a little dog he'd petted.

He was almost pleased by the short standstill on the bridge. That was the second bad sign. One more and he could pull out. But if there wasn't one, he would have no choice.

∽ 4 ∾

WHAT AN UNBELIEVABLE EVENING, thought the prostitute.

Indeed, almost every evening was remarkable in its own way in her line of work. She wasn't an ordinary prostitute. Sometimes she wondered whether she was one at all. If the main characteristic of her profession was offering sexual services, she did this only rarely. She didn't have sexual relations with most of her customers, at least not in the usual sense. And what they expected from her was not the usual perversity either. Theirs were very unusual desires. She fulfilled them without question and was amply rewarded.

Four times a week she went to regular customers in elegant city neighborhoods. On Monday she saw a polished elderly gentleman who greeted her in a wine-colored robe with a scarf around his neck, wearing leather slippers. He had two identical Siamese cats.

She undressed behind a screen and put on a one-piece bathing suit the same color as his robe, then tucked her hair into a bathing cap, climbed up a wooden ladder and got into a large tank in the middle of the spacious study. She spent twenty-five minutes in the heated seawater swimming mostly underwater, surfacing just to inhale.

Only the cats watched her. The man sat at his desk the whole time, his back turned to the tank, writing something quickly, almost frantically. She never found out what and wasn't even interested. At the end of the séance he would be waiting by the ladder, holding open a bathrobe, also wine-colored, before escorting her to the screen.

On Tuesday she visited a sculptress. She undressed to the waist and sat on a tall bar stool covered in black silk. The sculptress, dressed in dark-blue overalls, would start rapidly working in clay. Periodically she would raise her eyes toward the young woman. The work might last just ten minutes or more than an hour. At the end the prostitute rarely recognized herself in the sculpted figure. Usually she was unable to recognize anything, but was very careful that no judgment about the sculptress's work showed on her face.

This was not ordinary posing, however. After the sculpting was over, the young woman undressed all the way and went up to the stand where the sculptress worked. A large plate of beaten eggs was waiting for her there. She immersed her hands in them and then squeezed the figure for exactly three and a half minutes. The sculptress timed this with a stopwatch and put the deformed clay straight into the kiln.

Thursday was reserved for a painter. There were no paintings in his atelier because they didn't last long after he finished them. He didn't use a canvas and paint but a thin square wafer and spreads of various colors. The painting was already finished when the prostitute arrived.

She ate it fully dressed. He let out a cry with every new bite that disappeared into her mouth. As he did this, he tore off his colorful paper clothes piece by piece. By the end, the painter was bare, but the young woman quickly squeezed out what was left in the tubes of spread, covering his nudity.

On Friday she went to a composer's. Wearing nothing but an Indian headdress and a leather kilt, she slid under the piano where he was sitting. When he started composing, she plucked out one of the feathers from the headdress and started tickling the soles of his raised bare feet.

He had great stamina. Even though she tickled him relentlessly, he stoically endured up to half an hour. The atonal music was not to her taste, but she had high regard for his squeaky compositions owing to the torture that gave rise to them. When she emerged from beneath the piano, she always found him drenched in sweat.

She didn't work on Sunday, but accepted the new customer who'd been referred to her. If she'd had a chance to see him beforehand, she would have found an excuse not to go. She could put up with various shortcomings in men, but this one seemed to have acquired everything that turned her stomach. He was short, bald and overweight. When he opened the door for her and licked his lips, she almost turned on her heel and left, even though this would have seriously damaged her reputation.

She was certain he would lunge at her as soon as she entered. His bulging, watery eyes were simply burning with lust. But this didn't happen. He led the way to the parlor. Everything in the room was black, just like his suit, except for two bright red leather armchairs facing each other in the middle of the room.

He indicated that she was to sit in one of the armchairs while he sat in the other. All he did was look at her without speaking for a few moments. What happened next was the last thing she would have expected. He started to sing.

She had to close her eyes so the ugly would not clash with the sublime. The man's freakish looks certainly did not fit his divine voice. She soon forgot his disgusting exterior, enthralled by his dazzling singing.

The song ended suddenly with a rattle. She opened her eyes, which grew as big as saucers. At first it seemed that the redness of the armchair was spreading, absorbing him into it. And then she realized that blood was gushing out of his mouth and nose. The upper part of his chest was already soaked.

She abhorred the sight of blood. Drenched as he was, he appeared even more appalling than when she had first set eyes on him. It was impossible to believe that the mouth that had produced such a wondrous voice a moment ago was now a geyser.

She jumped out of the armchair. The man's horrified eyes pleaded for help, but she was too terrified to do anything. She rushed out of both parlor and apartment and tore down the stairs, taking two and three at a time.

She ran all the way to the distant intersection. She finally got sufficient hold of herself to realize that this would only draw attention. She slowed down, but additional willpower was needed to start walking normally.

The realization that she might be linked to the unfortunate man brought new disquiet. She hadn't left any traces in the apartment and no one had seen her running this late, thank heavens, but there was still the person who had recommended the ugly singer. She sighed with relief when she remembered that no danger threatened there. He too had secrets he didn't want disclosed.

She almost raised her hand to stop the taxi that had just appeared, but at the last moment decided to get a little farther away. She would take a taxi on the other side of the bridge.

 5

THIS IS MY CONSCIENCE, thought the thief on a bicycle.

Although he wasn't even twenty-five, he was already an experienced thief. He'd never been caught. And he'd never had a guilty conscience.

It was true that he stole, but he saw nothing wrong with stealing books. On the contrary, he considered it a virtue, like righting a terrible wrong. He took them from people who didn't read books and were often proud of it. Books had only monetary value for rare book dealers.

His operations were always carried out at night, by bicycle. He appeared harmless, like a student out late, for example. Even if the police had stopped and searched him, they wouldn't have found anything suspicious. All he needed to pick locks was the hairpin in his long blond hair tied back in a ponytail. That was enough to break into even the best protected expensive book storage. Were the police to find such a volume in his backpack, they'd take no notice. What could be more natural than finding books on a student? And could ordinary beat cops be expected to recognize highly valued collectors' editions?

He didn't keep the stolen books for himself. He took them to a library and left them without being seen. Periodically libraries would announce the inexplicable appearance of valuable volumes, but most often no one came to claim them. Books stolen by the young man rarely had owners who could prove their ownership.

This evening's operation had seemed routine at first. Nothing had heralded trouble. As usual, he'd made thorough preparations at home. The internet is a real treasury of information if you know how to search for it and if you understand the coded language of those who have reason to use it. He'd discovered the final destination of one of three remaining copies of a late fifteenth century book on alchemy. All he had to do was patiently wait until there was an opportunity to get hold of it. No one can permanently guard what they want to keep.

Just as he'd expected, the tall windows of the fourth-floor apartment were dark. He had no trouble opening the front door to the building, but the apartment door required some effort. It took him seven and a half minutes to attend to the four locks that the antique dealer believed were an impenetrable impediment.

Eleven minutes later he was standing next to the deep-pile rug in the living room that had been flipped back, in front of the open safe in the floor. He smiled, thinking of the lack of imagination of some thieves and their predictability when they had to safeguard something of their own from theft.

He took the book out of the thin plush-lined case and put it in the knapsack on his back. Then he closed the safe and put the rug back in place. Since the dealer was not inclined to read, he would have no reason to take out the book and would live for some time in the assurance that it was in his possession. When he finally found a buyer for it, a surprise would be in store.

As the young man was on his way out, he heard rustling behind the door to another room at the other end of the living room. He froze in his tracks and pricked up his ears. At first he thought it was an animal. If it was a dog, thank heavens the door was closed.

He continued toward the exit on tiptoes and then heard groaning behind him. There was no longer any doubt, a man was back there. He almost broke into a run to get out of the apartment, but a new sound stopped him. Right then he was ready to expect anything, but not music. Although subdued, he immediately recognized the opening bars of Bach's *Brandenburg Concerto No. 1*.

If it hadn't been this type of music, he would have obeyed the inner voice ordering him to scoot out of there. But curiosity got the better of inherent caution. Who was listening to Bach in a house where reading was disparaged?

He aimed the thin beam of his flashlight at the distant door and slowly headed in that direction. He pressed his ear against the smooth wood. If there were any other sounds in the next room, they were overpowered by the magnificent harmony of stringed instruments.

He turned off his flashlight, went down on one knee and peered through the keyhole. Most old houses in this part of Vienna still had heavy double doors with large keyholes.

He had a good view of the central part of the parlor, but could hardly believe the surreal scene before his left eye. An elderly man in a dark-blue pinstriped suit was climbing up a pyramid of books. Although the thief could not make out any details of the books in the stack, he concluded by their covers that they were old editions.

When the man climbed onto the flat top, he went partially outside the young man's field of vision; only the middle of his chest was visible. The Bach enthusiast raised his hands above his head and did something with them. Whatever it was, it didn't last long. They were soon back down by his sides.

If it weren't for the music, it would have seemed that everything behind the doors was on hold. The body without shoulders and head stood like a statue with its upper part broken off.

The suspense was finally broken by a motion that coincided with the culmination of the first movement.

Legs started to swing, books at the top scattered in all directions and the man's foothold disappeared. His body fell suddenly, bringing his shoulders into the thief's field of vision. When the trembling began, the young man jumped back from the keyhole. His flashlight clattered to the floor.

He knew he had to act quickly. Every passing second decreased his chances of helping the poor man in the parlor, but he was unable to move. He just stared at the door in disbelief. The coolheaded composure that was the pride of his thefts had completely abandoned him.

When he finally snapped out of his numbness, he turned and rushed outside without a second thought. He was already on the stairs when he realized he had to go back. Fortunately, in the midst of his urgency he hadn't closed the door all the way. It would have taken a lot longer than seven and a half minutes to handle the four locks in his present state.

As he bent down to pick up the forgotten flashlight, he was careful not to look at the keyhole.

He pedaled like a madman, wanting to get as far away as possible from the suicide's house. But increasing the distance did not bring the hoped-for relief. He had a sinking feeling he'd never felt before. He tried to convince himself that he'd done the right thing, that what had happened in the parlor didn't concern him; everyone has the right to do what they want with their lives, he would have been in terrible trouble if he'd gotten involved. His vague unease, however, was undaunted by these matter-of-fact reasons.

He recognized it as his conscience when it forced him to stop on the bridge.

∽ 6 ∾

THIS IS A MESSAGE FROM HEAVEN, thought the nun.

God sees everything, even what no one sees in the darkness of a movie theater. She shouldn't have lost sight of that. Now she would get the punishment she deserved. This was the message she had just been clearly sent.

The nun went to the movies every third Sunday of the month. Never alone, of course. She always went with another sister, but today her plans had almost failed because she couldn't find anyone to go with her.

The one who went with her most often suddenly came down with a high temperature. Of the other two who occasionally shared this tolerated foible, one couldn't go because her relatives had come to visit and the other wouldn't go because she didn't like horror movies, and one was showing that evening. There were other movie theaters in town, of course, but they only went to this one because it was the closest. All you had to do was cross the bridge.

She had already decided to spend the evening reading when the reverend mother summoned her unexpectedly. Although the nun hadn't requested it, she gave her permission to go by herself. Furthermore, she had nothing against the nun going to the ten o'clock show. If she'd been informed earlier that there was no one to go with her, the nun would have made it to the eight o'clock show.

Such kindness was not unusual. The reverend mother treated her charges with truly maternal care. She understood their needs and desires and was accommodating wherever it did not go strictly against the rules of the order. It was actually all the same to her if the young nun went to the earlier show in the nearby movie theater with another nun or to the later show alone. Nothing serious could happen.

And nothing did happen until the very end of the film, except for the fact that someone sat down on the seat next to hers after the movie had already started. She saw nothing suspicious about this because the theater was almost full.

She wasn't overly fond of such films either. She was more bothered by the loud sound that made her jump than what was on the screen. Indeed, the chills also filled her with a certain excitement, but she would never admit that, not even to herself. In any case, it would have been easier if one of her sisters had been there so she could hold her hand during the particularly terrifying scenes.

But just as the denouement started, a hand took hold of hers in her lap. She was so engrossed in the film that it took one or two moments before she realized it was the late arrival on her right. Shocked, she tried to wrench her hand away, but he held on tightly.

She was totally beside herself. She knew she had to do something, she couldn't leave her hand in his, but didn't know what. If she screamed, the other viewers might not pay attention, thinking she'd been frightened by the movie. She could stand and put up a fight. This would lead to a suspension of the show and inevitably cause a lot of commotion. That would put an end to the reverend mother allowing her to go to the movies, even with other sisters.

As she was feverishly racking her brain, the squeeze suddenly relaxed and the hand withdrew. But there was no chance to sigh in relief, because it came back. It no longer sought her hand but went down to her knee. The nun turned to stone. She wanted to pluck it off, but felt certain that wouldn't work. She was convinced that a powerful man was sitting next to her.

The paralysis remained even when the hand started sliding up her thigh. Now she had to do something even if it caused a scandal, but she still didn't move, letting the hand advance. The man on the seat next to her was no longer important. She could still win out over him, but not over what was in her head.

Just as with the chills, her feelings were twofold. The stranger's wandering over her body gave rise to both repulsion and pleasure. Loathing and excitement. She knew the former had to have precedence, she had not withdrawn to a convent without reason. Nevertheless, she wasn't the least surprised when the latter prevailed.

She closed her eyes and relaxed, no longer following the film. The sound even seemed quieter. Now it was as though a multitude of hands were moving over her, reaching every spot, even those that should be inaccessible while sitting.

She wanted this to last, but then remembered that the movie was almost over. This thought snapped her out of her lethargy. What would happen when the lights came on? He would have to stop touching her, that was clear, but then what? How could she look him in the eyes? What would she say to him? Should she pretend that nothing had happened?

She didn't have time to come up with any answers because something unexpected happened just then. The hand was no longer on her. She opened her eyes and briefly turned her head to the right in bewilderment. All she could make out in the darkness was a large outline. It looked somewhat strange, although she couldn't say what was wrong. It was as if the stranger were slumping forward.

Just then, through the sound which had grown loud again, she heard something like a hoarse rattle coming from the seat next to her. Disgusting egotist, she thought when she realized what it must be. That was why she detested men. They only thought of themselves.

She wanted to get up and leave so he would have no chance for further exultation when he saw a nun sitting nearby. But she was in the middle of the row, so it would be awkward. She had to be patient a little longer. She would leave as soon as the credits began, something that irritated her when other people did it, but she wasn't prompted by mere impatience.

As she watched the final scenes of the movie disinterestedly, she seemed to hear another hoarse rattling nearby. It must have been her imagination, those things certainly couldn't last that long.

The lights came on when she was already near the exit. She had no reason to turn around. She didn't know what he looked like so she wouldn't recognize him among the people behind her getting ready to leave the theater. He was certainly not the only large man there.

She turned around nonetheless.

A holdup was caused when she stopped, staring at where she'd sat. Several people were gathered around a seat, partially hiding the slumped form upon it. Before the stream of people pushed her out of the exit, she glimpsed the bent over usher as he stood upright and shook his head.

She almost ran out of the theater. Quickly moving away down the street, she was haunted by the feeling that someone would soon rush after her and accuse her of the stranger's death. It was not until she was near the bridge that she managed to convince herself that her fears were unfounded. No one would accuse her, of course. No one had seen anything in the darkness. Everyone would think that the large man had died of over-excitement. That happened in movie theaters periodically. People with weak hearts should not watch horror movies.

She would have returned to the convent untroubled if it weren't for the realization that came to her after stopping briefly in the middle of the bridge, seemingly for no reason.

There are eyes that see in the deepest darkness and culpability cannot be hidden from them.

7

WHEN THE PROMPTER GOT home, she first looked for the hedgehog. It was a real master of concealment. Her apartment wasn't big, but it still managed to find new nooks to crawl into. It was a good ten minutes before she finally caught sight of it in a shoe at the bottom of the closet. She'd left the sliding door slightly open as she was getting ready to go to the theater late in the afternoon.

She'd brought it home four and a half months ago from a walk in a nearby park. She hadn't wanted an animal, she knew nothing about hedgehogs, she didn't like his threatening quills and ugly snout, but how could she leave the poor creature on the path with a thin trail of blood behind him?

Even she was surprised at how quickly she'd gotten used to it. It wasn't demanding and she soon changed her opinion about the quills and snout. She learned how to pet its back safely and in the end found its little snout cute. She didn't hesitate to kiss it lightly.

Because she was lacking intimacy, she had no trouble convincing herself that the hedgehog returned her affection. She talked to it frequently, certain that it listened attentively. At night it slept next to her bed on a little pillow in a cardboard box.

The tenseness of the evening did not keep her from her customary reading before going to sleep. After putting the hedgehog in the box, she settled down in bed and took a large book from the bedside table. It was an illustrated edition of Japanese fables where many of the heroes were barbed.

Reading one fable out loud was usually enough to put the little hedgehog to sleep. This time, however, halfway through the story her own eyes started to close. She did her best to finish it, but couldn't. She apologized to the hedgehog, put the book on the bedside table and turned off the light with its green lampshade. She fell asleep almost the moment her head hit the pillow.

∽ 8 ∾

QUICKLY ENTERING HIS HOTEL room, the contract killer did not turn on the light right away. He took one step to the right of the door and stood leaning with his back against the wall. There was no reason for this. He hadn't seen or heard anything to alarm him. He always did this as a precaution. He could take nothing for granted. People in his profession most often came to harm when they let down their guard, thinking they were safe.

When he finally turned on the light, a clanking came from one end of the square table in the middle of the room. He smiled. The sudden light had caused the little brown hamster to run on the wire exercise wheel in its cage. He always took the hamster with him when he was on assignment. He believed it brought him luck.

On the table in front of the cage was a chessboard with the pieces set out. Almost all of them were still in play: only two white and two black pawns lay next to the board. The contract killer went around the table, stopped behind the cage and stared at the position. He stayed like that around three minutes and then moved the black knight.

He tapped the top of the cage lightly and moved to the opposite side of the table. He became absorbed again. This time in less than a minute and a half he moved the white queen from one end of the board to the other.

"Check," he said softly, raising his eyes to the hamster. The wheel did not stop turning.

The man spent the next twenty minutes in the bathroom. He got undressed and filled the sink with warm water. He took a little bag of laundry detergent out of his toiletry bag, poured it into the water and then added his underwear and socks. He washed them thoroughly, rinsed them, squeezed them out and hung them on the shower curtain rod above the bathtub.

He was just as thorough under the shower and then brushed his teeth at length. After he had put on his pajamas, he stood in front of the mirror for a moment and straightened his collar and sleeves.

Back in the room, he went to the small closet, opened the suitcase at the bottom and took out a book. He settled in bed, smoothed the cover and turned on the light on the bedside table.

Grabbing hold of the red linen bookmark, he opened *Crime and Punishment* approximately in the middle.

The moment he started to read to himself, the clanking on the table stopped.

He always read ten pages, but tonight he was already drowsy after the second. He closed the book, put it on the bedside table and turned off the light. He wondered whether this was a good or bad sign. Before he reached an answer, sleep got the better of him.

∽ 9 ∾

ALTHOUGH SHE HADN'T EVEN shaken hands with her customer that evening or touched anything in his apartment, the first thing the prostitute did when she got back from work was take a bath, as usual. She filled the bathtub almost to the top. As hot water poured out of the faucet, the bathroom filled with steam that fogged the large mirror.

She put in three different colors of bubble bath. There was so much of it that just a brief swish with her hand formed thick foam. When she slid into the bathtub, foam predictably overflowed, but she took no notice.

She lay there without touching herself, soaking in the water as the dissolved bubble bath entered her open pores and cleaned them. This usually took about fifteen minutes. Tonight she stayed in the tub almost twice as long. What she wanted to wash off was not merely physical dirt.

She would have stayed longer, letting out lukewarm water and adding more hot, if she hadn't been so sleepy. She bravely endured one full minute of stinging icy needles from the shower. She usually put the bathroom in order before leaving it, but this time decided to do it in the morning.

Before going to bed there was just one more thing

she had to do. She would not have skipped it even if she'd fallen asleep in the bathtub, because it gave her great pleasure. She went up to the large aquarium on the commode and took a spoonful of crumbly food from the can next to it. She watched with a smile as the greedy mouth surfaced and quickly caught the crumbs sprinkled over the greenish surface.

After its dinner was over, the prostitute pulled up the sleeve of her terrycloth robe and slowly slipped her hand into the water. It wasn't easy to catch the smooth, wriggling creature, but she'd acquired the skill long ago. When she finally had the long black eel between her fingers, a sensual prickling shot through her.

She was fond of it not only because of the sensual pleasure but also the kinship they shared. Both of them used their bodies to provide others with pleasure for the sake of the comforts they received in return. Her only hope was that the eel didn't feel about her what she felt about all her customers.

She took her hand out of the aquarium earlier than usual, then removed her robe and dried herself with it. She wore nothing underneath. She always slept naked. She put the robe on an armchair and quickly slipped between the satin sheets.

Her hand was already heading for the light on the bedside table when her eyes paused to consider the book next to it. She hesitated a moment, then picked it up. She would read at least one page. It had been a long time since she'd liked a novel as much as *Anna Karenina*.

When she put the book back on the bedside table a few minutes later and turned off the light, the bedroom did not sink into total darkness. It was disturbed at uneven intervals by a bluish, sparkling light from the commode. The effect was irresistibly lulling.

∽ 10 ∾

REACHING HIS APARTMENT, THE thief first took care
of what he'd stolen, as he always did after a theft. He
put on the plastic gloves he'd used in the evening's operation, took the book out of his knapsack and put it
in the last place one of his colleagues would look for it.

It was not likely that another thief would have reason to break in here. A garret studio in an unpreten-
tious part of town did not indicate any booty worth
the effort. If there had been anything valuable inside,
the owner would certainly try to protect it better. Even
someone who was not a thief by profession could easily
open the lock.

Should a robber enter the studio nonetheless, they
would never suspect where the valuables were kept.
There was no secret safe or hiding place and what was
out in the open appeared used, to say the least. Scant
furniture, a small television and a dusty computer that
no one would pay for.

Part of one wall was covered by a library, but it
contained only tattered old editions. A thief without
knowledge of books would take no notice. Should one
who was well-informed end up there, which was highly unlikely, after a cursory inspection they would conclude that the books were worthless. At least for those
who measure the value of books by money.

In order to establish that this was not the case, they
would have to examine the library carefully. And
thieves, those with and without knowledge, don't have
time to check over three hundred books. Where better to place a fabulously valuable book than among a
multitude of cheap ones? Furthermore, it wouldn't be
there very long. The young man would wait a week and

then take it to a large library. In the meantime, it was perfectly safe on the shelf.

After the book, it was time for his bicycle. The thief spent fifteen minutes cleaning, lubricating and fine-tuning it. He never failed to do this every evening. He spent at least eight hours a day on the bicycle at his delivery job. It had to be reliable.

He spent much less time on his personal hygiene, barely two or three minutes in the bathroom. He scrubbed his hands thoroughly but only splashed his face lightly with water and went over his teeth once with a toothbrush. In the end, he stripped down to his underwear.

Just as he slipped under the thick blanket, there was a scratching at the window. The young man smiled and got up. It hasn't been here in at least two weeks, he thought. He opened the window a crack and gazed at two tiny eyes on the end of a bare branch of the tall chestnut tree.

The previous spring he'd found the squirrel in his apartment when he got home from work. He'd left the window ajar and the leafy chestnut almost entered his room. The little animal was terrified, unable to get its bearings and escape. He pretended he hadn't seen it, however, so it sneaked through the window after he'd opened it wide, but stayed on the closest branch, looking into the room inquisitively.

Weather permitting, he would leave the window open and a handful of hazelnuts on the inside sill. They were gone in the evening. Over time, the hazelnuts were waiting for the squirrel farther and farther from the window, but that didn't stop it from taking them.

The first time it scratched was in the middle of a summer storm that woke him during the night. Still sleepy, he didn't realize it was the squirrel and thought branches were scraping the window. The origin of the insistent sound finally dawned on him, so he rushed to open the window a little. The squirrel hesitated and then dropped to the windowsill. Most likely it would have stayed there if a sudden clap of nearby thunder hadn't forced it to jump to the floor. It did not leave the room until the next morning when the storm had passed.

Before long the squirrel started visiting him at night without any reason. It didn't hesitate to enter if the window was open and when autumn arrived and he started closing it, the squirrel would announce itself with a scratching, asking to be let inside. He was usually already asleep, but the squirrel kept it up until it woke him. Then the young man would leave the window ajar, even if it was cold, so scratching wouldn't wake him again at the crack of dawn when the squirrel had a mind to leave.

Now, after opening the window, he went back to bed. The squirrel hopped over to the desk and stared at him intently. Never before had it examined him so carefully. He felt uncomfortable under such probing scrutiny. Stretching out his hand, he turned off the light on the wall above the head of the bed.

He tried to go to sleep but his thoughts kept returning to the incident in the parlor. Some ten minutes later when it was clear the sandman wasn't coming, he turned on the light. The squirrel was nowhere in sight. He couldn't hear anything, but that wasn't unusual. It moved without making a sound.

He picked up a paperback copy of *Confessions of Felix Krull* from the floor and opened it to the place where he'd turned down the corner the night before. He was convinced that he wouldn't be able to read in such a troubled state, but it was better to stare at the book than into the darkness.

After the very first paragraph, however, the horrible haunting sight through the keyhole started to fade. By the time he had finished the page, nothing weighed heavily on his mind anymore. He yawned, folded the corner of the next page and then hit the light switch a third time.

∾ 11 ∾

As soon as the nun returned to the convent, she got out of her long black dress. She had to give it in to be washed without further ado. She felt that traces of large male hands could be seen all over the cloth. Particularly where they least belonged.

She spent a long time under the shower. She didn't like touching herself so she just surrendered to the cold, sharp stream of water, as though doing penance. When she left the bathroom, shivering in her warm nightgown, she felt cleansed externally more than internally. One shower, regardless of how long and how cold, was not enough penitence for her twofold sin.

She knelt before the crucifix in front of the bed, head bowed, hands clasped, and sank into prayer. She did her best to be as ardent as possible, but something was missing in the words she whispered. They were unable to express what was troubling her. The best thing would be to talk everything over with the reverend mother the next day. Even if the nun didn't express herself properly, she would probably understand her better than the one she was now addressing.

She got up, crossed herself and went to bed. She

thought of turning off the wall light right away, but knew she wouldn't be able to fall asleep, agitated as she was. What if she read a little? She looked at the dark cover of the Bible next to the brass cross on the bedside table and wondered which part to select. What wisdom from the holy book would be able to calm her now? But perhaps wisdom was not the remedy for her malaise. She needed something for her heart, not her head.

She was still deep in thought when a squeaking sound came from the corner across from the bed. She sighed. This night full of unusual events had put it completely out of her mind. She quickly got out of bed, went to the table and unwrapped a napkin. It contained a small piece of yellow cheese that she'd sneaked out of the refectory, as she did every evening.

Smiling, she headed for the corner carrying the cheese in the palm of her hand. She sat on her heels and put her hand to the floor. The white mouse with eyes like two tiny bright red rubies didn't budge as she approached it and stretched out her hand. Before it set about eating, it looked at her briefly. The ends of its long whiskers twitched slightly.

It had appeared the very first evening after she'd moved into this room three and a half months ago. The sister who'd been there before her had gone into hospital and never returned, so she didn't know whether the mouse was indigenous. It probably was and her late sister, like her, had hidden the fact that she was sharing her room.

The squeaking had terrified her the first time she heard it. She'd sat up cautiously in bed and stared fearfully at the rubies embedded in snow-white fur. If she hadn't been afraid to get up, she would have followed her instinctive reaction: rush to find help. The convent caretaker would have easily gotten rid of the little mouse. But the longer she looked at it, the less appealing was the thought of the old man taking it out crushed in a mousetrap or poisoned.

She'd examined the whole room carefully the next day, but couldn't find where it was coming from. There were no holes in the walls or floor, or at least none that she could see. The mouse would simply appear, seemingly out of nowhere, when she got ready to go to bed. It would squeak and stay in the corner.

Two days later she realized what prompted it to come out of its invisible hiding place. That evening she'd given it the only thing she had to eat: a little sugar. The next day she brought it cheese for the first time.

In the beginning she left it in the corner and then something occurred to her that required twofold courage: hers and his. Would it eat out of her hand? Tremendous willpower was needed to stretch out her hand slowly and great hunger was all that stopped the little mouse from slinking off. This is what it did, nonetheless, as soon as it got hold of the little piece of cheese.

It took two weeks for the mouse to realize there was no reason to run away. But more than two months of patience and persistence were needed before it finally let her pet its back cursorily as it ate. She couldn't tell whether it liked it but the touch of the soft smooth fur on her fingertip brought almost sensual pleasure.

As she petted it now, watching it gobble up the late cheese, the tension inside her subsided. When she soon returned to bed, she was convinced she would easily fall asleep. Even so, a little reading would be an additional help. She turned toward the bedside table, but did not take the black book on it. She reached for the lower of the two drawers and took out a thick volume with a cheerful cover. *The Charterhouse of Parma* was the right reading for her tonight.

∾ 12 ∾

THE PROMPTER WAS WALKING across the Yellow Bridge. She hadn't gotten very far when she wondered where she was going. This was the way she went to the theater, but rarely on foot, and certainly never this late. She didn't know the time. The night must be well along. The bridge was completely deserted like this only in the wee hours.

Just then she caught sight of someone in a dark rain-coat in the middle of the bridge, their back turned. She hadn't seen them earlier because they were standing by the railing in the gloom between two lampposts. She thought it was a man staring at the Danube. He didn't seem menacing, but she still thought it would be best to go back. She had nothing to do on the other side of the river at this late hour.

She turned around and gaped in astonishment at what she saw. Several steps behind her began a void that went all the way to the bank, as though someone had cut off fifty meters of the bridge with a huge knife. She had no idea what had happened to the missing part. It was unlikely to have fallen into the Danube, she would have heard the splash.

There was no going back; her only choice was to continue toward the other end. Just as she started walking, a frightening thought crossed her mind. Had the bridge begun to collapse? She didn't understand how it could so soundlessly, but it might be possible. She didn't know anything about collapsing bridges. She ran as fast as her legs would carry her. Would she be able to reach the other bank? Just look at the trouble a person gets into by being where they don't belong in the middle of the night.

She crossed the next fifty meters and then her intuition told her to turn around again, without stopping. Her presentiment was right. Another section of the bridge had been cut off. This is terrible, she thought. She would not turn around anymore.

Although she was beside herself, she hadn't completely lost her self-possession. She had to warn the stranger on the other side of the danger. He was still gazing unsuspectingly at the river, oblivious to what was happening. And no wonder when not a single sound disturbed the peaceful night. Then her piercing scream broke it.

The man turned around as though she had addressed him softly. That's when she noticed the leash in his left hand. A small dog was standing by his feet. Since she was already close to the middle of the bridge, she recognized that it was a Pekingese. Without dropping the leash, the man applauded as he watched her run.

What a strange fellow, she thought. That's the type that hangs out on bridges at night. Nevertheless, she had to warn him. She tried to shout that he should get away too, but the running had left her breathless. She couldn't get a word out, so she waved her hands, pointing behind her back.

The man nodded his head and pointed to the opposite end with a smile. At first she thought he was asking whether he should run that way too. She nodded, but he didn't get going. He just stood there smiling idiotically, his hand pointing down the bridge.

What's so funny, she wondered, and when she finally looked in that direction, she stopped dead in her tracks. Just barely ten steps in front of her, everything was gone. She spun around swiftly and saw the same thing on the side she'd come from. The bridge had collapsed simultaneously at both ends. Only the small central part was left.

Terrified, she stared at the stranger on the upstream side. He was still smiling and had started clapping again. This infuriated her. His delight will be short-lived when the last part of the bridge disappears, she thought. Indeed, she didn't know how it was still standing. There were no pillars. Better not go into such matters. Bridges weren't her forte.

When something started coming out of the pavement in front of her, she thought it heralded the end. The middle of the bridge was about to fall silently into the river. She didn't know how to swim and even if she did, she wouldn't enjoy swimming in the icy water. Did she dare hope that this idiotic guy would come to her rescue? What if he didn't know how to swim either, or what if he saved the little dog first? That wouldn't have surprised her. Dog owners were like that. The only thing they thought about was their pets.

Luckily, the moment had not arrived for the middle of the bridge to collapse. This realization brought relief, but there was no time for a respite. She jumped back a step before what was coming out of the asphalt. The strangest sight in the world could not have rendered her any more terrified. After what she'd already been through, she was ready for just about any wonder on the Yellow Bridge, but not for something quite as mundane as this.

She rarely saw the prompter's box from above. Now she was standing in front of it like an actor on a stage. It was illuminated but no one was inside. The applause from the other side of the bridge grew louder. She raised her eyes when she heard yapping. The Pekingese had gone up on its hind legs and was batting its front paws together, imitating clapping. She shook her head in reproach. She didn't approve of training animals.

Her attention was drawn to the box again. Someone had appeared inside. An unknown man in a dark-red robe with a scarf around his neck and rubber bathing cap on his head was holding a sheaf of papers. He leafed through them quickly. Since she was quite close, she saw that they were densely written pages in small, regular handwriting. Reaching the end, the man shrugged his shoulders with a rueful expression on his face. He signaled with his hand for her to wait and disappeared down below.

She thought he would be right back, but an enormous squirrel appeared in his place. The prompter backed away again, although not as far as she had the first time. She liked squirrels. She wasn't aware that they came this big, but why not? Dogs came in different sizes too.

The squirrel knocked on the metal edge of the box, then picked up a book and started to read in a soft voice. The prompter was not very surprised. If dogs can clap, why shouldn't squirrels read? They weren't any less intelligent than dogs. On the contrary. And they didn't need to be trained. They learned everything by themselves. Just like hedgehogs.

After the first sentence the squirrel stopped reading and gazed questioningly at the prompter. The prompter returned the questioning look. The squirrel quickly raised its paw to its mouth and turned it back and forth. The prompter was horrified. It didn't expect her to recite the text, did it? After all, she wasn't an actress.

Seeing her hesitate, the squirrel motioned with its paw over its shoulder to the opposite side of the bridge. The prompter looked that way. The man was now holding the Pekingese in his arms. There was a gaping void on the spot where the dog had stood. The man's legs had also disappeared to the knees. Like the last part of the bridge, he had no support either.

When the squirrel started reading softly again, the prompter grudgingly agreed to repeat the text. She already recognized the book. She didn't know that the Japanese fables had been dramatized, but she thought they were well suited to it. If they were staged in a Viennese theater, she would sneak the hedgehog in to watch the show. It would certainly be pleased.

The squirrel stopped after just two sentences and then motioned with its head. The prompter looked across the bridge again. The man's legs were gone. She wanted to signal to the squirrel to ask what came next, as actors did when they got stuck, but the squirrel was going through something under the box. Finally it brought out a new book.

The prompter repeated the famous first sentence of *Anna Karenina*. She overemphasized, like poor actors do. Her eyes were glued to the man without legs. She stopped speaking at the beginning of the next sentence because the torso lost its stomach right before her eyes. First he raised the dog to shoulder level.

Then everything happened quickly. After the introductory sentence of *Confessions of Felix Krull*, his chest disappeared. The dog was moved to the top of his head. The beginning of *The Charterhouse of Parma* took his shoulder and neck. Only the hands held the Pekingese above his head.

What was the squirrel doing, wondered the prompter. If this had happened to her, she would have been fired on the spot. If the squirrel was working as a prompter, why hadn't it prepared properly? How could it search for the text of the play after the performance had already begun? No wonder they were losing the audience.

Out of the corner of her eye she noted something moving. She turned around and saw one end of the small portion of remaining bridge vanish into thin air. It disappeared as though a giant eraser had rubbed it out with sweeping movements. The same thing happened to the other end. Soon there would be nothing left.

She looked wild-eyed at the box and saw the puzzled squirrel open a new book. She didn't wait for it to start whispering because she suddenly realized what was playing on the Yellow Bridge that night. Of course, she should have thought of it immediately. Actors can only depend on themselves onstage. Clumsy prompters are useless.

The first sentence of *Crime and Punishment* stopped the erasure of the bridge. The second brought back the man's neck and shoulders, the third his chest, the fourth his stomach, the fifth his upper legs, the sixth the rest of his legs. As she spoke the seventh, the arms raised above his head slowly lowered the dog to the pavement. Four more sentences were needed to bring back the parts of the bridge that had vanished. The two banks were joined once again.

Thunderous applause rang out. The man cheered and the Pekingese hopped on its hind legs. The prompter hesitated just a moment and then bowed deeply. She had always imagined this moment. She envied the actors so much at the end of the play when they bowed to the audience. No one ever thought of her then, although she deserved the most credit for everything turning out well. The actors could rely on her completely. She would never leave them in the lurch like the stupid squirrel that was no longer in the box. She hoped it ended up in the Danube.

The applause went on and on and when it finally stopped she had no trouble imagining that the curtain had dropped for the last time, although it was not there. She left the stage beaming with joy, heading toward her bank on the bridge that had regained its sturdiness.

∽ 13 ∾

As soon as he stepped onto the Yellow Bridge, the contract killer realized that something unusual was happening. There was a table in the middle of it. Someone was sitting on the opposite side, his head resting in the palms of his hands. He was looking intently at something on the table in the gloom between two lampposts, so the contract killer had to strain his eyes to discern what had drawn the man's attention. Fortunately, his eyesight was still excellent. How else could he do the job he did at his advanced age?

He'd seen chess being played in various places—he personally played wherever he happened to be—but never on tramway tracks in the middle of a bridge. Although he was indeed surprised, it didn't seem inappropriate. He wasn't biased. Why not play it here? The trams stopped working at midnight, so no one would bother the solitary chess player until morning.

The contract killer immediately took a liking to the man. He knew what it was like not to have an opponent, so you played against yourself. Perhaps the man would buy a hamster too. Or some other small animal, it didn't matter. Another presence at the table made solitary games easier. He wondered whether the man would move to the other side of the table after he made his move. That also helped if you didn't have a partner.

But now there was someone else! Of course! He was there! What was more natural than for two chess players without opponents to join forces? Even though it was already late, he would really enjoy a game. Indeed, there was only one chair, but it didn't matter. He wouldn't mind standing. He walked briskly toward the middle of the bridge.

As he got closer, he had a better look at the person on the other side of the table. The man in the black suit was overweight and bald. If he stood up, he would probably be short. Had the contract killer been a woman, he would have been repulsed and perhaps even disgusted by him. But as a man he was indifferent. He couldn't care less what his opponents looked like. Most great chess players were ugly anyway. He couldn't remember a single one who was handsome.

He stopped in front of the table and looked at the board. One glance was all he needed to see that something was wrong, but it took a few moments before he realized what it was. The black pieces currently being played by the man were ordinary. The same could not be said for the white. He'd seen all kinds of pieces but never any that were alive.

Sixteen ruby-eyed white mice were standing on their hind legs on various squares. They were wearing white coats with the name of the piece written on the back in back letters. The king and queen were wearing yellow crowns. The mice were standing calmly for the most part with a few slight movements here and there.

The contract killer wondered in bewilderment how the man dealt with the white pieces. Did he pick them up and move them like he did the black pieces or did he somehow induce the little mice to move to another square? An answer was forthcoming. The white bishop on a dark square moved diagonally to the left side of the board without any external inducement.

So the man was not playing against himself as the contract killer had mistakenly assumed. The mice were his opponent. And by no means a weak opponent. The move that had just been played contained many hidden dangers. And generally speaking, black was not sitting well, although the game had only just started. All the pieces were still on the board.

The ugly man placed his forehead on the tips of his outstretched fingers and became lost in thought. He clearly understood he was in trouble. Indeed, there was a life-saving move that the contract killer, as an experienced chess player, had already seen, but he would not interfere in the game. He was always terribly irritated when bystanders failed to control themselves.

Around two and a half minutes passed in dead silence and then a woman suddenly stood up straight behind the man's back. The contract killer scolded himself. He hadn't noticed her crouched there in hiding. His guard was down, which was not good. It might have been someone intending to kill him.

The woman was wearing dark-blue coveralls and was holding a piece of clay that she quickly started to shape. The chess player did not turn to look, but the contract killer stared at her nimble fingers in admiration. The formless mass turned into a human figure before his eyes. He should have realized who it was before the little bust was finished, but sometimes it is hardest to recognize oneself.

He was tempted to applaud the sculptress' skill, but she didn't share his enthusiasm. She crossly smashed the clay flat and threw it over the railing into the Danube. Before she dropped back down behind the chair, she took out an egg from somewhere and cracked it on her head. As she sank down, the egg yolk and white dribbled over her face.

Who can understand artists, thought the contract killer with a sigh and returned his attention to the board. The chess player had just made his move with a knight. Wrong, the bystander wanted to say, but held back. Now he would lose a pawn.

And indeed, the next moment the mouse playing the role of the white castle lunged at the undefended black pawn. It put its little paws around the thinnest part, lifted it with some effort, took it to the edge of the board and put it on the table. As it returned to the place where the pawn had stood, the other white figures gave a resounding, squeaky congratulation.

Just as the sound died down, someone started to appear behind the man's back again. The contract killer assumed at first that it was the woman coming back to sculpt him in clay again, but instead there appeared an enormous white mouse. Standing on its hind legs, it was a head taller than the sitting chess player. Its front paws were holding a large mug full of red liquid.

It bent down over the man and put the mug in front of him. The man shook his head briefly, but the large mouse paw resting on his shoulder quickly broke his weak resistance. He took the mug, gazed into it with disgust and then brought it to his lips. Just then the contract killer smelled something he recognized immediately. No wonder. It was the trademark of his profession.

He's not going to drink that much blood just for losing a pawn, is he? The contract killer's face contorted into a grimace as he watched the thick sticky liquid pouring into the poor man's mouth. Some blood dripped down his chin and onto the black shirt and black jacket. The spot that spread there looked like a red bib.

After the repulsive drink was downed, something like ululating came from the board. The big mouse raised the empty mug, bowed deeply and then sank behind the chair with a beaming face.

The man took out a black handkerchief and wiped his bloody chin. He hesitated briefly about whether to do something with the stain on his chest, but left it. When he turned his pale face toward the board, everything was crystal clear to the contract killer. No one in his state would be able to continue the game. Inevitable defeat awaited him.

What fate was in store for losing the game, when he paid so dearly for the loss of a pawn, wondered the contract killer. No, this could not be permitted. He didn't approve of bystanders getting involved, but now he had to interfere. The circumstances were exceptional. He would teach the mice a thing or two about playing chess.

The ugly man reached for the knight to make a new move, but was interrupted by the contract killer who cleared his throat softly. The chess player caught the bystander's eye and stretched his hand toward the castle. The white pieces raised their heads reprovingly to the contract killer, but he pretended not to notice. He didn't say a word, so they couldn't accuse him of anything.

Seven more moves followed, guided by his eyes, before the mice started fidgeting on the board. They dropped down on all fours and looked at each other, mystified. The game that had seemed already won was lost. The squeaking now expressed anger at their defeat.

The big mouse came up again with a mug full of blood. It gave the contract killer a dirty look, closed its eyes, and started drinking, spilling a bit on its chin too, so a rosy bib covered its white fur.

After the mouse had set down the empty mug, it held onto it a few moments, eyes closed, shaking its head. When it opened its eyes, the mug was the first thing to fly into the Danube. It hesitated a moment and then rushed after it, powerful hind legs easily flying over the low railing. No splash was heard up above.

The mice instantly scattered in all directions. They left their white robes behind them on the board like empty casings. Two crowns rolled down the pavement with a clatter.

The contract killer bowed silently to the chess player whose face had regained its color. He received a bow in return and a grateful smile. When the contract killer headed back, he received another sign of gratitude. The singing of a divine voice accompanied him to the end of the bridge.

∽ 14 ∾

WHAT AM I DOING on the Yellow Bridge so late, wondered the prostitute. She wasn't an ordinary streetwalker. And look at how she was dressed. Where had she found that garish red suit made of artificial leather? Or the fishnet stockings? Had she walked all the way here in high heels? And just look at the disgusting little black vinyl purse. There was certainly a mirror inside but she wouldn't take it out, not for all the world. She could imagine how overly made up she was with such an outfit. Thank heavens her regular customers didn't go to such places at night. Her reputation would be completely ruined if they saw her like this.

She was standing in the middle of the bridge in the gloom between two lampposts. Her elbows and lower back were leaning against the low railing. Her left leg was slightly bent at the knee. What a nice pose, she thought. If anyone passed by, they'd know at once who they were dealing with, even without a two-bit hooker's outfit. She straightened up. She'd better leave this place before someone came along.

Just as this crossed her mind, someone appeared at the left-hand end of the bridge. Since she was nearsighted, she couldn't make them out. Only now as she looked into the distance did she realize she wasn't wearing her contact lenses. Why was that? She never went out without them when she was working. Even though she looked good in glasses, she'd stopped wearing them. It turned off her customers. She only put them on if they specifically asked.

Something was moving toward her down the middle of the tramway. What could it be? They didn't make cars that small and no motor was humming, there was just the clattering of wheels. Like someone was pushing a cart.

She would have preferred not stay to see what it was, but now she had no choice. The only way to avoid the encounter would be to head toward the right-hand end of the bridge, although she had nothing to do on that side. But she wasn't likely to get there first. She could barely walk in these high heels and didn't feel like taking them off and walking on the cold wet pavement in porous stockings.

All that remained was to wait there until the vehicle passed and then leave. She turned toward the river to be as inconspicuous as possible. She might be taken for a weirdo and people usually left them alone. Pretending to gaze at the dark surface of the water, she listened intently as the wheels drew near.

She froze when the vehicle stopped at her back. She kept her eyes turned forward, waiting. Nothing happened. No one addressed her or came up to her. Several long, tense minutes passed before she finally turned around. She couldn't spend the whole night staring at the Danube.

What she saw was more puzzling than frightening. The cart was like a square wooden box with large wheels on either side. It was being pulled, not pushed. The elderly man in a dark-blue pinstripe suit did not seem a fitting draft animal and the noose around his neck was even more incongruous.

The other end of the rope was in the hands of an enormous hedgehog. It was sitting upright in the middle of the heap of books that filled the cart to the brim. When it saw the prostitute looking at them, it pulled lightly on the rope.

The man went to the back of the cart obediently and took out a thick old-fashioned book with a gray cover. He went up to the prostitute and held it out. She vacillated a bit before accepting it and raised it toward the left lamppost so she could read the title.

She gave *The History of Prostitution* back to the man

with a huff. No one had yet openly insulted her like that. Prostitution was the last word her distinguished customers mentioned in her presence. Not only out of consideration for her but out of self-respect. Just look what happens when you're judged by the clothes you wear.

This time when the noose tightened around the man's neck, he jerked and rushed to the cart to take another book. It was also an old volume with a light-brown cover. Even more irritated, the prostitute pushed away *Great Courtesans* and turned toward the river. This really was going too far. She wouldn't give them another chance to humiliate her.

She would gladly have shown her back to them if she hadn't heard a gurgling behind her. She looked over her shoulder and saw the man on his knees. His eyes were as big as saucers as his fingers tried in vain to release the squeeze of the thick rope so he could get some air. The hedgehog had viciously tightened the noose.

The prostitute kneeled down next to the man and tried to help him. In her anger, she had mistakenly thought he was the hedgehog's accomplice. Are accomplices tied with a rope? The brutal hedgehog treated the man like a servant. Or even a slave.

The noose relaxed as soon as she put her hands on it. The man took a deep breath, stood up and gave the young woman a grateful look as he helped her up. He went straight to the cart and this time brought her an old edition in a green binding.

She didn't give back the copy of *The World's Oldest Profession* right away, but asked by sign language what was expected of her. He held out his open hand. She looked at the hedgehog in disbelief. Did he really think she was going to pay for the new insult? Just as she shook her head in anger, the rope started to tighten.

Eyes flashing, she stuck her hand into her little purse. She didn't know what was inside it. She always had enough money on her, but streetwalkers kept only small change because they were frequently robbed. She felt several coins at the bottom.

She took one out and placed it on the man's palm. He sighed and went up to the cart. When the hedgehog saw how much it was being paid, it let out something that sounded like a snort and its quills bristled.

Doesn't like it, eh? Well, take a look at this. With a broad smile, she threw the green volume over the railing. She'd paid for the book fair and square, she could do what she wanted with it. She looked defiantly at the dumbfounded hedgehog and then beckoned to the man and he came at once. She poured all the coins from her purse into his hand.

He soon returned from the cart carrying a dozen thick books. As she threw them one by one into the Danube, she felt not the slightest regret. She suspected that the old volumes were quite valuable, she could have kept them and resold them, earning a nice profit, but watching the infuriated hedgehog gave her infinitely more pleasure.

When the last book ended up in the river, she felt frustrated. She wanted to continue, there were a lot more books in the cart, but no more money in her purse. As triumph returned to the hedgehog's face and the rope tightened again, she suddenly had a flash of inspiration. Perhaps she was not without money. Purses were for small change, while streetwalkers kept their earnings in a safer place.

She reached into the plunging neckline of her artificial leather suit and felt folded bills between her breasts. She removed them with a broad gesture, went up to the hedgehog and stuck them into his hand. She motioned to the man to stand aside, went around the cart and started throwing books into the dark abyss under the bridge. As she watched them fly over the railing, for the first time she felt true delight in the work she did. The rattling sounds made by the hedgehog as it shrank in size with every disappearing volume only increased her satisfaction.

The man went up to the cart when there was nothing left inside but the hedgehog, now a normal size. He didn't look vindictive as he picked it up by the quills and took it to the edge of the bridge. When he opened his fingers, his expression was that of a man getting rid of something very dirty. He rubbed his hands together and took the noose from around his neck. He rolled up the rope and just dropped it over the railing.

He smiled at the prostitute and opened a little door at the back of the cart. He held out his hand to help her on. He would take her home. That was the least he could do for her. How could he let a lady suffer walking on such tall thin heels?

∽ 15 ∾

THE THIEF WAS SURPRISED as he rode his bicycle over the Yellow Bridge. He passed by there periodically at a late hour and everything was always empty. Rarely did he come across a tardy passer-by. Now something was happening on the upstream side. A large man was standing in front of a stall between the two middle lampposts, looking at what was on display, illuminated by two red lanterns. The sides of the stall hid both the objects and the seller.

What could this be? Were they opening a night flea market? That would be great. He loved to visit places where used books were sold. He'd bought several rare editions dirt cheap. Unfortunately, his delivery job let him go to flea markets only on Saturday and Sunday. He'd certainly missed a lot the other days. If they worked at night, he could stop by almost every day.

As he started pedaling faster, he wondered what was for sale on the first stall of the market. He would be delighted if it turned out to be second-hand books. Lady luck was not smiling on him, however. When he stopped in front of the stall, the smaller of the two curiosities attracted his attention first.

Above it was written in yellow letters outlined in black: "Second-hand Sexual Aids." Of course, thought the frowning thief. His intuition had failed him. He should have realized as soon as he saw the red lanterns. Would a bookseller choose such lighting, even at a night flea market? Furthermore, who would sell books here when they couldn't expect any customers? People on bridges at this hour didn't care about the joy of reading. They were lured by other pleasures.

The bigger curiosity was the seller. He looked like a giant brown hamster. The thief had never seen such a convincing disguise before. Looking at it from a distance of twenty meters, he would have sworn that it really was a blown-up rodent. No wonder the stall owner went to such efforts to hide his real face. His nighttime activities would certainly detract from his daytime reputation.

I should watch out for my reputation too, concluded the thief. Although it was late, someone might appear and recognize him. He met a lot of people as a delivery boy. Better leave right away. There was nothing for him there anyway. He wasn't interested in sexual aids. Particularly not second-hand.

His foot was already back on the pedal, ready to ride on, when the only customer picked up a book from the counter. The thief's foot returned to the pavement. He hadn't suspected books to be among the sexual aids. The fact that they were second-hand only increased their value in his eyes. He looked toward one end of the bridge and then the other. No one was around. He wouldn't stay long, just look at the titles. Rare editions turned up in the most unexpected places. He got off his bicycle, leaned it against the railing and crossed to the other side.

First he took a closer look at the seller. It wasn't a disguise after all. There was a real hamster behind the counter. Dealers in suspicious goods had really lost all sense of proportion. If mischief-makers like that started using the wonders of genetic engineering, where would it all lead? The hamster looked tailor-made for the job. It bowed cordially to the new customer. Although it didn't say anything, the thief wouldn't have been surprised if it had spoken.

There were no books among the variety of used objects on the counter. The large man was holding the only one. He probably won't buy it, hoped the thief. He would wait to take a look at it if the man put it back. To hide his impatience, he started looking at the goods on sale with feigned interest.

He never would have imagined all the things that were considered sexual aids. What, for example, were the little blacksmith's bellows used for? Or the violin bow? And what about the nutcracker and grater? How was a wire bottle brush used? Or a three-pronged rattle? He had to let his imagination run free to think what could be done with a Christmas tree star and opera glasses. He didn't even try to imagine what several items could be used for because he had no idea what they were.

He reached for the book as soon as the customer put it down on the counter. After leafing through it briefly, he put it down too. He'd stayed for no reason. The edition was worthless as far as second-hand books were concerned. It seemed to have strayed there. What sexual aid could be provided by *The Illustrated Ascetic Handbook*? Human sexuality was indeed hard to understand. Judging by its tattered state, the thin volume had been frequently used.

As the thief headed for his bicycle, he was stopped by the sound of air being exhaled. He turned around and saw the large man blowing through his cupped hands. The hamster smiled and nodded its head, then bent down under the counter. It took out something that looked like a colorful crumpled plastic sheet. It felt around a bit and then pressed on one spot.

The sheet started to inflate at the same moment. The shapeless pancake soon took on solid form. In less than ten seconds the hamster was holding a doll in the form of a young woman. She was wearing a fire-fighter's uniform with a helmet on her head.

The man eyed it briefly and shook his head. Still smiling, the hamster stretched its hands across the counter and opened them. The doll began to go up like a released balloon. The customer and thief followed it with their eyes until it soon merged with the darkness above the bridge.

The seller bent down under the counter again and took out a new sheet. The customer didn't like the second doll either. The doll in the form of a young woman chimney sweep with sooty cheeks also floated up into the night.

When the third sheet inflated, the thief looked in bewilderment at an unexpected shape. This wasn't a doll in the shape of a young woman but of a middle-aged painter. His naked body was streaked with paint. He had a palette and brush in one hand and a square wafer with various spreads on it in the other. He brought the wafer to his mouth every now and again and bit off a little piece.

High technology isn't lagging much behind genetic engineering, thought the thief in admiration. If a doll can eat, who knows what else it's capable of doing? They probably make such improved female models too.

Without waiting for the customer to decide, the hamster let the painter follow the first two dolls. It even gave it a push. The expression on its face was articulate: "Sorry, my mistake." A drawn-out shriek followed the painter until he disappeared into the darkness.

The customer gazed at the fourth doll somewhat longer. Regardless of how twisted it was, the thief liked the female cop best too. Although he had no need for such aids, when the customer shook his head again he almost asked to take it.

The smile had left the hamster's face when it reached below the counter for a fifth time. Sellers have a hard time with picky buyers, thought the thief. He wouldn't have the patience for this line of work. Selecting from among the stock took longer this time, as though the hamster was searching for something special.

The thief sighed as he looked at the nun doll. Suddenly everything was clear. No night flea market would be opened here. The stall would be on the bridge just this night, to satisfy secretly the needs of real perverts. The things on offer here could not be purchased even under the counter in official shops.

He was convinced that the hamster had finally guessed

the large pervert's hidden desire. His head would finally nod. But he was wrong. The man stared for a few moments at the doll dressed in a habit. Then he grabbed the left side of his chest, stood there without moving for a moment or two and collapsed on the pavement.

The thief looked at the seller, who wouldn't even dream of helping the customer. On the contrary, the hamster started giggling as though something amusing had happened. The laughter suddenly stopped when it brought its hand to its own chest, felt around briefly just like with the plastic sheet and then pressed approximately in the middle.

The thief was startled. It wasn't going to inflate too, was it? It was already enormous. How much more could it grow? Geneticists should be reined in before their experiments got totally out of control. He took two steps back, but there was nothing to fear. The hamster started to shrink, not grow.

There was a hissing sound like letting air out of a beach ball, and then not only the hamster but the entire stall and everything on the counter began to deflate. It all took place in an instant before the eyes of the flabbergasted thief. He blinked just a few times and three dimensions became two. Now there was a colorful wrinkled sheet instead of the stall. Although there was no wind, it fluttered, rose up just enough to go higher than the railing and slipped over it.

The thief was curious to see it end up in the Danube, but just then the large man groaned on the pavement. He'd forgotten about him, preoccupied as he was with the disappearing hamster. Panic filled him. What should he do? He wasn't in the least skilled in first aid and no one else was on the bridge.

He had a fleeting thought that perverts didn't deserve first aid, but scolded himself at once for this unworthy consideration. What if he'd misjudged the man? He too might be a random passer-by caught by the sly hamster in its trap. When he'd set eyes on the nun doll, it was not lecherous arousal but shock that caused the heart attack.

The young man feverishly tried to remember what to do in case of a heart attack. In his disarray, the only thing that came to mind was artificial respiration, but the thought of giving mouth-to-mouth to a man horrified him. He shook his head briskly. He could never do it, even at the cost of having this stranger on his conscience.

He had started walking backward, retreating toward his bicycle, when he suddenly stopped in mid-step. Of course! There was an elegant solution. He could give artificial respiration without putting his mouth anywhere near the man's. He turned around, ran to his bicycle, took his pump and went straight back to the poor man on the pavement.

Touching his mouth could not be avoided, but he could bear that. He put the head at the end of the thin hose into the man's mouth, held it in place with one hand and briskly pushed the handle of the small bicycle pump with the other.

The first flow of air into the man's lungs brought a change. His eyes came to life and focused. After the second, his round face turned ruddy. After the third, he tried to speak, but the thief shook his head and pressed the pump head more firmly into his mouth.

After the fourth injection of air, the thief almost dropped the pump as he jumped up. The body had risen horizontally about one foot from the pavement, as though helium had been pumped into his belly. The man's beaming face, however, indicated that he was feeling fine.

The thief hesitated briefly and then continued pumping. But he managed to press the handle just two more times. The man reached his waist with the first and was a little above his head with the second. Then the pump head fell out of his mouth because the thief could no longer reach it. Stretching out his arms, the young man feared he would not be able to hold the heavy body when it started to fall without new air.

But the body neither fell nor stayed there hovering. It continued to rise as though it had more air than it needed. As the thief watched in amazement, the man turned face down. It seemed he would say something, but in the end he only waved with both hands. As the thief returned the greeting down below, darkness swallowed up the large figure.

The thief returned to the other side of the bridge one more time. He put the pump back in place and mounted his bicycle. Before leaving, he looked about the empty bridge. How strange, he thought. It's as though nothing happened.

∽ 16 ∼

THE NUN HEADED ACROSS the Yellow Bridge with quickened steps. She had to get back to the convent as soon as possible. The reverend mother would be very disappointed. She had completely betrayed her trust. There was no excuse for such tardiness. If only she knew where she'd been until then. It certainly wasn't somewhere decent. Such places weren't open in the dead of night. What time was it anyway? It must be very late since everything was so empty.

As she approached the middle of the bridge, she saw that she wasn't alone on it after all. A gray-haired man in a raincoat with the collar raised was standing on the other side, his back turned. She hadn't noticed him earlier because he was stock-still. From a distance he appeared as one with the railing in the gloom between two lampposts. At first she thought he was looking at the river, but then she noticed that he was holding a fishing pole. What normal person goes fishing in the middle of the Danube at night, she thought. She bowed her head and walked a bit faster.

Just after she passed him, the man suddenly spoke in a deep voice. If she hadn't recognized it immediately, she would have taken to her heels without a second thought. As it was, she stopped, turned slowly and stared in disbelief at the figure on the upstream side. Viewed from the back, she still would not have guessed who it was, but did anyone else have such an exceptional voice?

What was he doing on the bridge at this late hour? Indeed, why did she find this strange? Undoubtedly he'd gone out after the performance to relax a little. An actor's profession is very tiring and stressful, and he was not a young man anymore. Why shouldn't he fish, even in the middle of the night if it did him good, and still give his heart and soul to acting? Was he bothering anyone here?

He was her favorite actor. Whenever the reverend mother let her go to the theater, she would try to watch his plays. Once the reverend mother had smiled and reproached her that if he wasn't so old she might think the nun was in love with him. And she was in love with his masculine bass that the years had done nothing to change. A chill would go down her spine when she heard him onstage.

Both his voice and what he was saying sent a chill through her now. It was the famous monologue from a tragedy. She should know which one, she'd seen them all several times, but her memory unexpectedly failed her. That must be punishment for staying outside the convent so late.

But if she hadn't, would this exceptional privilege ever have been hers? Had she ever dared to hope that she would be the great actor's only audience? It was as though he was performing just for her. Indeed, he didn't realize she was there. It was questionable whether he would continue if he knew she was behind his back. She had to remain silent. This made her uncomfortable, as though she were doing something improper, and her conscience kept reminding her of the reverend mother, but how could she resist the temptation?

The monologue broke off in mid-sentence when the bell on the top of the pole rang out. The actor quickly started to wind the little reel. What a time for a fish to bite, thought the nun, irritated. If he'd continued just a little longer, she would certainly have remembered the play. It was on the tip of her tongue.

When he reeled in the line, however, there was neither a fish nor a hook on the end. A brown hamster was wriggling there, tied around the waist. Questions washed over her. What was a hamster doing in the river? Who tied it with fishing line under the bridge? What would happen to it?

The answer to the last question was all she received. The actor untied the little rodent and caught it by its short tail. He threw back his head, raised the hamster and started lowering it into his open mouth. The terrified nun watched in silence as the animal struggled in vain. It didn't stand a chance.

She covered her mouth with her hands so she wouldn't scream and vomited. How awful! And how terribly fooled she'd been! Another repetition of what followed her like an affliction. Whenever she was attracted to a man, sooner or later he always turned into a monster.

She had to get back to the convent as soon as possible. The world outside its walls was full of horror at night. Just as she took a step, the bass voice boomed on the bridge once again. As though bound by the invisible threads of some force, she stopped and turned toward the old actor just as he lifted the pole above the river again. She knew she had to feel loathing for him, but his voice seemed to have enchanted her.

He started a new monologue. She'd listened to this one often too. There was no time to remember where it was from because the top of the pole started ringing after the third sentence. This time she didn't recognize the catch right away. The line ended with some sort of little black ball. The actor cautiously tried to take it in his hand, as though it might harm him. She understood why he was reluctant when he finally caught several quills between his thumb and index finger.

He won't, will he, thought the shocked nun, seeing him raise the hedgehog above his head. The loathsome pig will have a hard time with this one, she hoped. Serves him right. May it perforate all his intestines. But no painful grimace deformed the old man's face. On the contrary, he chewed with an expression of bliss, as though the softest and tastiest morsel was in his mouth.

As soon as he had swallowed the hedgehog, he quickly cast the line without a hook over the railing. The very same instant he started his third role, so she had no time to think about leaving. She must know which play this was from, the words welled up from her memory a moment before he spoke them, she could have recited the monologue herself, but the title escaped her. This was quite frustrating, so she was relieved when the bell started ringing after the second sentence, much louder than before, even though this announced a new horror.

Now it could be heard as well as seen that he'd caught something big. The fishing pole bent almost in two and the actor leaned all the way back, struggling with might and main to wind the reel. He made slow progress, so a fair amount of time passed before something took shape from the depths. It was not until a man's head was well above the railing that the nun made out what it was.

She could no longer suppress her cry. The actor didn't turn around at the muffled exclamation since he was preoccupied with pulling in his new catch. Did his depravity know no bounds? He not only devoured live animals but was a cannibal as well. How could he eat a whole man? He wasn't a python. She put these thoughts aside for the moment. She had to do something to prevent him. She couldn't just stand there and watch.

As she was feverishly devising a plan, the man emerged to his waist. He wasn't tied like the hamster and hedgehog. One hand was holding onto the taut fishing line and the other held a large colorful feather. The reeling in suddenly stopped and nothing happened for a moment or two. And then the acrobatics began.

The man turned upside down. His torso was below the railing and his legs were up above it. Although he was properly dressed, he wasn't wearing shoes or socks. He bent his left leg at the knee and the hand with the feather came up from down below and tickled the bare sole. The laughter that echoed was melodic, like a composer checking the sound of a cheerful *passaggio* that had just crossed his mind.

This irritated the actor for some reason. He released the reel in anger and it spun out of control. The legs disappeared instantly and a splash was soon heard from the Danube. The nun sighed. Better for the poor man to drown than be eaten. And he might save himself if he knew how to swim.

The fourth monologue lasted for just one sentence before the bell rang, so the nun didn't reproach herself for not recognizing the play. What difference did it make anyway? This monster didn't deserve to have his roles remembered.

The actor was still fuming, so he wound the reel more briskly than usual. He took no pleasure in the new catch. Instead of lifting the tiny squirrel over his head and slowly lowering it, he just stuffed it in his mouth and swallowed without chewing.

After the actor waved the fishing pole and jerked the line toward the river, there was no chance to start the fifth monologue. The bell rang while the reel was unwinding. He gazed at it in bewilderment and then started to reel in the catch.

Since there was no voice to keep the nun there, she headed along the bridge dejectedly. This was the story of her life. Everything always ended in massive disappointment. It would be best not to leave the convent anymore. She wouldn't miss the movies and the theater. Books were enough for her. They wouldn't let her down.

If she heard the beginning of another monologue, she would keep going undeterred. The force no longer held sway over her. What she heard, however, was not the powerful voice of the actor but the rattling cry of an old man. Curiosity made her turn around.

Coiled around the actor's chest were four rings of a black snakelike body that gleamed a bluish color every now and then. It must have been squeezing tightly because his face was distorted in pain. His hands were close to the last catch, but he didn't have the courage to touch it, clearly afraid of an electric shock.

Although her faith had taught her that gloating was a mortal sin, she succumbed to its pleasure without remorse. The actor more than deserved the torment. He'd devoured poor creatures from the Danube while sullying high-minded monologues that he used as bait. Now the river was getting its revenge.

But the longer she watched the old man's agony, the less vindictive she felt. He needed to be punished, but not this brutally. Even the worst criminals had the right to compassion and who else, if not a nun, could be expected to give it? And the sooner the better, because if she hesitated any longer it would be too late to atone for her sins.

She ran to the actor and grabbed the slimy eel without a second thought. Her body clenched in expectation of the electric shock. There was one indeed, but to her complete bewilderment she was filled with bliss instead of pain. At its peak, the title of the play from the first monologue flashed from her memory like lightning. She couldn't hold back the cry of joy and didn't want to. The moment it escaped from her parted lips, the pressure eased up on the first black ring around the old man's chest.

Reaching for the subsequent rings, she tried to convince herself that compassion still prompted her and the flashes of pleasure were just incidental rewards for her resuscitated memory. Three more cries came in quick succession at the discovery of the buried titles and each one loosened the next ring.

After the last one relaxed, the eel fell limply off the old man's body onto the pavement. It quickly slid through the railing and disappeared into the darkness under the bridge. No sound came from down below.

The nun and the actor stood there a few moments facing each other in silence, marked by the traces of their efforts: panting, flushed faces, sweating. Radiant.

Then he offered her his arm. She took it and they headed toward the end of the bridge. If anyone else had been on it, they would have heard two voices alternating, male and female, turning a notable monologue into a dialogue. But who else would be on the bridge deep in the night?

∽ 17 ∾

WHEN THE LOW MORNING sun flooded the Yellow Bridge with light, two gazes were drawn to the spectacle in the middle. One came from an upper floor of a nearby skyscraper and the other came from the deck of a boat approaching the bridge as it sailed down the Danube.

The voyeur generally watched the river and its bank at night. He had binoculars with night vision making it possible to see almost as though it were day, but circumstances had prevented him from satisfying his passion the night before. Whenever that happened, he was haunted by the feeling that he'd missed something important.

The entire stretch of the riverbank and particularly

the bridge and its vicinity became irresistibly inviting as soon as it got dark. He'd seen just about everything there, watching stealthily and with great pleasure. It seemed as though everything that was eccentric and perverted in Vienna converged on this place. There must have been a show the night before too.

The bridge was least interesting in the morning. Early trams transported innocuous citizens who never suspected that an entire parallel night world had recently been there. The voyeur raised his binoculars, hoping his experienced eyes might find some trace of it. . . .

Only one passenger went out onto the boat's deck so early. The boat had been due to reach Vienna late the night before but as soon as it got dark they'd put ashore somewhat upstream. An ambulance and police car met them at the pier. The former left with its siren howling as soon as they put someone on a stretcher inside it. The latter, with two inspectors in civvies and two uniformed policemen, stayed until after midnight. When they left, they took someone from the boat with them. The captain apologized to the passengers for the unexpected delay, but was not specific about what had caused it. He only mentioned "unforeseen circumstances."

At first the passenger was disappointed at not being able to see Vienna's nighttime panorama from the river, something he'd been looking forward to. But since he was a cheerful man at heart, he didn't let the bad mood take hold. He could easily make up for what he'd missed another time, and this way he actually came out ahead. Many night cruises were available on the Danube, but it was questionable whether they were organized in the early morning. And Vienna must have its charms at daybreak too. Who could tell what interesting things awaited him. . . .

The voyeur realized at first glance that the five men he'd spotted in the middle of the bridge didn't belong to the daytime world. They were standing side by side next to the railing, looking nonchalantly upstream. People who were rushing to work right now didn't have time for such idleness.

The gray-haired man in a raincoat with the collar raised seemed familiar. Of course! Of all public figures, actors visited the bridge most often at night. He'd watched the old man in a television series but couldn't remember his name. The owner of the Pekingese next to him bent down to the little dog in his arms periodically and whispered something to it. In the middle was a short, fat, bald man. His blood-red bow tie was all that disturbed the blackness of his clothes. The voyeur usually saw men like that hiding in the bushes along the bank, shamelessly spying on lovers. The fourth was an older man in a dark-blue pinstripe suit. He was swinging a thick rope that was hanging over the railing. The last one was a large middle-aged man. His big hands had a firm hold on the railing, as though he wanted to tear it out.

A wave of frustration swept over the voyeur. He couldn't get over the fact that trivial obligations had deprived him of a unique treat. Something that might appear once in a lifetime. Never before had it been so exciting on the bridge in the morning. He could only guess what had happened the night before. And there was no excuse for it being gone forever. He felt like opening the window and throwing the binoculars at the river.

The passenger smiled when he spotted the men on the bridge above as the boat was about to go under it. He'd been told that Vienna never sleeps, but who would have thought it would be so lively in the middle of the Danube at this early hour? He would have to come back again soon and see the city at night. It would certainly be a unique experience.

He waved back to the five men who were waving to him in unison. He wanted to shout, "I'll be back soon!" but couldn't because the boat started gliding under the metal arch of the bridge just then.

Hands still in the air, the five men turned toward one of the skyscrapers in a row. They turned their eyes to the same window near the top and started waving once again. Then they dispersed. Two went to the left side and three went to the right side, looking downstream.

Third Wonder
Red Bridge, Bratislava

ON SUNDAY AT 20:43, Isaac, chilled to the bone, pulled an empty cart over the ice back under the Red Bridge in Bratislava on the left bank of the Danube.

"Nothing," he said apologetically.

Fyodor put down the book he was holding toward the fire. He could barely see well enough to read. Only tiny flames were flickering on the last half-burned log. His thin, frayed coat did not keep him very warm. He'd wrapped a shawl around his face to protect his ears from the cold. Most of his fingertips were sticking out of his torn woolen gloves.

"That's bad news," he replied with a hacking cough.

He was sitting on one of two dented beer kegs. The rest of their furniture was made of rusted barrels. They lighted their fire in the cut-off lower third of a medium-sized barrel and slept in two large barrels, placed on their sides. Isaac's barrel had a lid and Fyodor had put a plastic cover over his, held down by bricks.

They'd inherited all of this from the unknown homeless who'd lived under the bridge the winter before. Isaac had got there first at the beginning of fall.

That gave him the privilege of choosing which barrel to sleep in. The lid on his had three holes drilled into it for air. When it got cold he closed one, and when it began to freeze he closed another. Indeed, this did nothing to ease the cold, just as Fyodor was none the warmer for covering his opening with a tattered mattress he'd found.

∽ 2 ∾

Fyodor had arrived about ten days after Isaac. In the meantime, three homeless had tried to move into the other barrel, but Isaac had refused them all because Pascal didn't like them. The tiny dog had growled as soon as it set eyes on them. The dog's disapproval was unlikely to have been decisive if Isaac's large stature and frown hadn't gone along with it. And the large switchblade he happened to have in his hand.

Pascal spent most of the time under Isaac's old army coat. The little dog was almost hairless, so as soon as it turned a little cold it trembled out in the open. Only its head protruded from the opening between the top two buttons of the army coat. Isaac also liked the warmth of Pascal's body, particularly on cold nights. It was like having a hot water bottle on his chest.

When Fyodor turned up, Isaac felt Pascal's tiny tail briskly wagging under his army coat. His decision to take him as a roommate was also influenced by the only belongings possessed by this thin, short, unshaved middle-aged man with thick glasses: six novels by Dostoyevsky. That's how he got his name. They didn't use their real names there. Their entire past stayed buried in the world they'd left in order to withdraw under the bridge.

Fyodor named Isaac for the apples that fell on his head sometimes. Isaac must have eaten something else when he went out, because he didn't lose weight, but on the banks of the Danube he ate nothing but apples. He would bring six of them. Like a passionate smoker, he would bite into a new one without properly finishing the first. He wouldn't stop until he had finished them all. Pascal received a small piece of each one.

Isaac carried out a little ritual before he started a new apple. He rubbed it thoroughly on his left sleeve until it shone, threw it into the air and then caught it in his mouth. He had a wide jaw so he usually made it. When he didn't, he punished himself by tossing the apple into the Danube, regardless of how crisp and juicy it was.

Isaac offered fruit to his roommate, but Fyodor's sensitive stomach couldn't take the apple's acidity. All he seemed to eat was zwieback. If he did eat something else when he wasn't under the bridge then it wasn't very nourishing because he'd visibly lost weight in the two and a half months he'd been there.

∽ 3 ∾

EVEN THOUGH THEY WERE free to do whatever they wanted, living together brought several obligations. They talked them over without many words, almost tacitly, because they were implicit. One of them was not to leave their habitation empty, if possible, so that other homeless wouldn't think it had been abandoned and move onto the left bank. If that happened, they would get their habitation back in the end, but not without a clash, and this way that could be avoided.

There was no danger of anyone stealing their things. When you have very little, you are protected from thieves. Fyodor's books were their most valuable possession, but thieves were not likely to be interested in them and would probably throw them into the river in frustration at the lack of booty, although what they expected to find among the homeless it was hard to say.

On the rare occasions when both of them went out, Fyodor would take the books with him just in case. Even though they weren't light, he maintained it was no trouble. Isaac had recently begun to lighten his load by taking the book he was reading.

More than a month and a half had passed before Isaac asked Fyodor if he'd lend him a book to read. He'd hesitated to ask, convinced that the books were his roommate's mementos and he would not loan them to anyone. He was surprised when Fyodor was delighted with his request.

He asked which book Isaac wanted to borrow. Isaac was embarrassed to admit that he had no idea because he'd never read anything by Dostoyevsky. Fyodor replied with a smile that in truth he was reading him only now. This was the only time anything about his past was mentioned. This was the fourth time he was reading Fyodor Mikhaylovich. It seemed, however, that all the previous readings were worthless and that here under the bridge he had truly come to understand the great writer.

∽ 4 ∽

UNTIL ISAAC HAD READ his first novel, they rarely talked. When the past is left out, not many topics remain. The present required just a few sentences and the future not even that much. With the exception of Isaac's periodic whispering in reply to Pascal's whining as he petted his snout, they spent most of their time in silence. Fyodor would read and Isaac would do some carving.

He would cut a piece off a branch they'd brought for firewood and patiently shape it. Sometimes the figurines he made were recognizable and sometimes they weren't, but they were all beautiful. Fyodor would frown at what Isaac did when they were finished, but never objected. First he gave them to Pascal to sniff them properly and then he went to the riverbank and placed them on the surface of the water, watching with a smile as the river carried them away.

The conversations about what they'd read became increasingly extensive. Isaac held back at first, fearing that he would look foolish, but Fyodor did nothing to show that his collocutor was out of his depth. On the contrary, he acted as though he was taking part in a serious literary discussion. As often as not he praised Isaac for his insight.

When they started talking about the other books, Fyodor became conscious of something that he'd previously overlooked. Isaac spoke to him as though Fyodor was the author of the work they were discussing. He felt awkward about openly drawing Isaac's attention to the fact that he didn't deserve such an honor, so he tried to do it in a roundabout way, but without success. All he could do was get into the spirit of Fyodor Mikhaylovich. He felt only a slight prick of his conscience when he soon began to enjoy the role.

∽ 5 ∾

AFTER THEY WENT TO bed, through the hole in Isaac's lid he would see the lighted slit between the edge of the plastic cover and the rim of the other barrel's opening.

For a long time he thought that Fyodor was reading by candlelight. Snow had already started to fall when he finally figured out what was actually going on. The secret was revealed by the dilapidated green folder that Fyodor kept with him always, just like the books.

Isaac was convinced that it held documents. In winter the police almost never checked under the Red Bridge. If they did, they went easy on homeless with an ID. He didn't understand why Fyodor used a folder for something that was more suited to an inside pocket and safer there, but didn't ask him because questions like that were not asked under the bridge.

Were it not for Isaac's excellent eye, he would have failed to note the folder's changes. It wasn't easy to perceive that it was becoming gradually thicker, as though Fyodor was adding a document to it every day, even those days when he didn't go out from under the bridge. Finally it dawned on him. They weren't documents. Fyodor was adding pages that he wrote at night.

Isaac already respected Fyodor and this discovery filled him with both admiration and pride. He was close to a writer who was creating a new work. It was almost as though he too were taking part. There might even be a place for him in the book. This would be nothing unusual, since all the books by Dostoyevsky he'd read so far were filled with the insulted and humiliated. He was dying of curiosity, but refrained from asking Fyodor anything. He would probably let Isaac read the manuscript when it was finished.

∽ 6 ∾

IN THE BEGINNING THEY both took care of the firewood. When the weather was dry, they would go on alternate days to a nearby park where they gathered dry leaves, branches and pine cones that had fallen off the trees. They brought them back in Isaac's two-wheeled cart. The park guard looked on indifferently, not so much out of consideration for the homeless as the fact that they did his cleanup work for him.

After the rain started it became harder to find fire-wood. The leaves were wet and didn't burn easily and there were fewer and fewer fallen branches so they had to break them off the trees. The guard chased them out for that even though they only chose dry branches on old trees.

Fyodor had no trouble gathering firewood on the ground, but he had a terrible time breaking branches. After being out a long time he would come back with scratched hands and slim pickings. Isaac finally gave him his knife to make it easier. He did it reluctantly, sensing trouble. And it happened the very first time. Fyodor soon came back under the bridge with an empty cart and a deep cut on the palm of his hand. Isaac was barely able to stop the bleeding.

After that, Isaac went out for firewood by himself. There was nothing else in the park but healthy trees and if he cut them, the guard would have the police breathing down their necks. He brought whatever would burn: old newspapers, cardboard and wooden boxes, sawdust from carpentry workshops and dis-carded combustible material from construction sites. If he got lucky, he would take two or three logs from a woodpile.

Unlike weekdays, it was much harder to find fuel on the weekends. Almost all the places Isaac went were closed. He tried to bring as much as possible on Friday, but however much he gathered there was usually nothing left to burn on Sunday evening. They could make it to Monday if it wasn't too cold, but if the days were frosty they had a whole night of shivering awaiting them when the temperature dropped very low. It was no coincidence that most frozen homeless were found on the first morning of the week.

~ 7 ~

Isaac had gone out in search of firewood at around seven thirty in the evening. He knew there were slim chances of finding anything. This Sunday that was drawing to a close had been one of the coldest days of the winter. Ice had studded everything and the north wind was howling mercilessly, reaching all the way into the shelter under the bridge.

Nevertheless, at least he had to try. Fyodor's cough was getting more protracted and hacking. The upcoming night might be fatal for him. And if that happened, then a great work of prose would remain unfinished. Isaac did not doubt that the green folder contained a great work. What else could it be if it came from Fyodor's pen? And not only a great work but one that might even have Isaac in it.

As Isaac went back under the bridge with an empty cart, he thought about what emergency measures he could take. If he had an ax he would no longer hesitate to cut one of the trees in the park. If the police arrested them, at least they would be put in a warm jail. But he couldn't do anything with just a knife.

There were other ways to end up in jail. The easiest would be to break a shop window and wait for the police. But somehow he was certain that Fyodor would not agree to that. Someone who reads Dostoyevsky might become homeless but not a lawbreaker. He most likely wouldn't let Isaac take him to the hospital either. They would have to admit him and even if they discharged him the next day, hopefully it would be a bit warmer. He had to persuade Fyodor somehow. That would go against the unwritten rules of life under the bridge, but what was the point of rules if there was no more life?

∽ 8 ∾

THERE WAS NO CHANCE to propose anything. After saying, "That's bad news," to the fact that Isaac had not brought anything to burn, Fyodor got up, closed his book, removed the cover from his barrel and went inside. He soon came out with five books in his arms.

"This will keep us warm tonight. If it's not enough, you'll have to add the book you're reading."

Isaac stared in disbelief at the books and then at Fyodor.

"You're not serious, are you?"

"Why not?"

"But they're books. . . ."

"They're just paper. And dry at that. They'll burn really well."

Isaac shook his head.

"Not just paper . . . Those are great works. . . ."

"Copies of great works. Reproductions. They're worth little more than the paper they're printed on."

"You can't look at it like that. . . ."

"If I bought this edition tomorrow in a bookstore, I'd have the same thing I have now. It would be like nothing happened."

"But there would be . . . Burning. . . ."

Fyodor struggled with a cough for a good minute before replying.

"Not every book burning is a barbarous act," he said in a subdued voice. "Some are justified."

"Burning Dostoyevsky can't be justified."

"Not even if it means saving someone's life?"

Isaac blinked at him for a few moments without speaking.

"But it's such a shame. . . ."

"It's a much greater shame when you let the little wooden figurines you carve float down the Danube. They are unique."

"They're just ordinary carvings. They can't be compared. . . ."

"Beautiful carvings. Works of art."

"If I'd known you liked them, I'd have given them to you. I'll carve you one tomorrow."

The new coughing fit lasted even longer.

"If we don't burn Dostoyevsky, you might not have anyone to give it to."

"That's not the only way to make it through the night. The hospital is well heated. Or the jail . . ."

This time hesitation postponed his reply.

"I'd rather not have anything to do with the police," said Fyodor at last, barely audibly.

Isaac said nothing in return. He just nodded his head and went to his barrel. The sixth volume by Dostoyevsky soon joined the others in Fyodor's arms.

∽ 9 ∾

"HAVE YOU EVER BURNED books before?" asked Isaac after Fyodor had placed the volumes on the keg where he was sitting.

"No."

"Then you don't know how they burn."

"What's there to know?"

"Maybe they don't last very long. It was you who said dry paper burns really well. We wouldn't accomplish a thing if they go really fast. We'd be burning them in vain."

"They'd quickly burn if we tore them into pages. But if we put them in the fire whole, they'll probably last as long as a log."

"It might not happen like that."

Fyodor started coughing again.

"It might not, but we have no choice," he groaned after catching his breath.

Isaac went silent again, blinking.

"What order will you burn them in?"

"Does it make any difference?"

"Maybe it does," he replied more softly than before.

"Do you have a suggestion?"

Isaac's eyes showed that he was giving the matter careful thought, but in the end he just shook his head.

"Then we'll go in the order we have here."

Fyodor took the book that Isaac had just brought from his barrel.

"Please don't start with *The Idiot*," said Isaac before Fyodor put it in the fire.

"Why?"

"I haven't finished it."

Fyodor looked at Isaac askance. He seemed about to say something, but changed his mind and put *The Idiot* on the other end of the keg, then took the thickest book out of the middle of the stack.

"You've finished this one."

"*The Brothers Karamazov* should come at the end."

"Why?"

"You told me it was his last novel."

"What's that got to do with it?"

"It makes no sense to burn the last book first."

Fyodor sighed and put *The Brothers Karamazov* on top of *The Idiot*. He took *The Possessed* from the bottom of the stack.

"You've read this and it's not the last."

"It's not the first either. . . ."

"So, do you want the first?"

The Possessed was put on *The Brothers Karamazov*. The new stack of books was now taller than the old.

"He wrote this one the first of all six," said Fyodor after taking *Notes from Underground* from the top of the now smaller stack.

"It's the thinnest."

"So what?"

"It'll burn the fastest."

"So let it burn the fastest."

"Maybe it would burn more slowly if it came after a thicker one."

Fyodor lightly hit his left palm several times with the slim volume of *Notes from Underground*. He finally put it on *The Possessed*, then picked up the two books remaining from the first stack and raised them head-high.

"Here, these are neither the thinnest nor the thickest, neither the first nor the last. Which will it be: *Crime and Punishment* or *The Raw Youth*?"

Undecided, Isaac's blinking eyes slid back and forth between the books. Fyodor suddenly started coughing. The hacking sound seemed to come from the bottom of his lungs. He covered his mouth with the back of his right hand without putting the book down.

"Well?" he asked in a weak voice when the coughing finally stopped.

Isaac shrugged his shoulders with an apologetic look.

Fyodor put the two books on the new stack and then picked up all six volumes. He looked at Isaac reprovingly and shook his head. Then he dumped the entire armful over the red-hot log without a word.

   10

SOME FIFTY MINUTES LATER, only scattered tongues of flame rose from the burned paper.

"It's over," said Isaac, speaking first.

Neither one had spoken while the books went up in a blaze. They didn't even sit on the kegs to warm themselves better. They stood with bowed heads, staring at the flames devouring the volumes, as though attending a cremation. Fyodor's sporadic coughing was all that disturbed the silence.

"I'd hoped they would last longer," said Fyodor.

"You shouldn't have put them on all at once."

"What's the difference? Even if I'd put them on one by one, they wouldn't have lasted any longer."

"Maybe, but we could have stopped after the first. We wouldn't have put on the others if the first one burned real fast."

"Why didn't you choose the one to start with?"

Isaac raised his head and looked at Fyodor.

"Why did you leave it to me to choose? It wasn't fair."

"You asked me about the order. I thought it meant something to you. It was all the same to me. And even if we'd stopped after the first one, we'd be in the same situation we are now."

"It wouldn't be the same. We would have kept five books by Dostoyevsky."

"A lot of good they'd do us while we froze."

"If I have to freeze, I'd find it easier not to have burning Dostoyevsky needlessly on my conscience."

Fyodor opened his mouth to reply, but coughing prevented him again. It took some time before he got his voice back.

"You won't freeze," he said at last, almost in a whisper.

~ 11 ~

FYODOR WENT INTO HIS barrel again and came out right away.

Isaac stared in disbelief at the green folder in his hand.

"What are you planning on doing with that?"

"Keeping you warm."

He raised the folder above the barrel with the smoldering black remains of the books, but before he dropped it, Isaac grabbed hold of the other end.

"You've lost your mind. You're not going to keep anyone warm. The pages will burn in an instant. You can't do that."

"Why not?"

"Why not? Because a manuscript is unique. It's not . . . a copy . . . a reproduction. You can't buy another copy tomorrow in a bookstore."

"Your carvings were unique too, but they floated down the Danube."

"That's not the same thing . . . This is a great work. . . ."

"How do you know?"

"I just know. It has to be. . . ."

"Great or small, it's mine. I can do with it what I want."

"It's not just yours. . . ."

"What do you mean?"

"I was close by when you wrote it. . . ."

"That doesn't exactly make you the coauthor."

Isaac lowered his eyes.

"Maybe I'm in it somewhere. . . ."

Fyodor stared fixedly at him for a few moments.

"Maybe. And maybe I was on some of the carvings that floated away. Was I?"

Blinking again, Isaac gave a barely perceptible nod.

Fyodor tried to say something, but coughing prevented him. Without waiting for the fit to pass, Isaac started talking rapidly.

"I was embarrassed to give you the figurines with your face. I'm not an artist like you, Fyodor. I'm just an ordinary homeless under a bridge. It's not fair to get back at me by destroying the only work of art that testifies to my existence. It will be like I never lived."

Fyodor finally spoke, but Isaac didn't understand.

"Come again?" he asked.

"I'm not Fyodor," repeated Fyodor in a tiny voice.

"It makes no difference. You're a great artist to me. Please don't burn the manuscript."

Fyodor's cracked lips turned up into the shadow of a smile.

"I couldn't even if I wanted. Manuscripts don't burn."

Isaac gazed doubtfully at the haggard face in front of him.

"So why are you holding it over the fire?"

"I told you. To keep you warm. All of us. Believe me."

Isaac wanted to believe him, but words alone were not enough for him to loosen his grip. It was not until he felt a slow movement around his heart—a little tail wagging under his army coat—that he let go.

The green folder started falling toward the remains of the fire at the bottom of the barrel.

∽ 12 ∾

A MYSTERIOUS OCCURRENCE UNDER the bridge was noticed on Monday morning. The young man who'd gone out early in spite of the cold to run along the left bank of the Danube could tell from a distance that something was unusual. He would always shiver when he went past the homeless who lived there in winter. Spending the night out in the open in such cold without any heating had to be terrible.

They certainly weren't cold now. Flames were belching out of a barrel where they'd lighted a fire, reaching almost to the lower part of the bridge. But why were they wasting the heat? There was no one nearby warming themselves. Perhaps they were still sleeping in the two barrels laid on their sides? So who was keeping the fire going?

He could have kept running like he did every morning, with just a slightly guilty conscience because he was unable to help the homeless, but curiosity got the better of him. He stopped and headed cautiously toward their habitation. He started feeling the heat some ten steps away. They've really got a good fire going, he thought.

He couldn't decide how to address them. He'd never spoken to any of the homeless before. He might not have to now either if they were sleeping. That would be best. He would just take a look to make sure everything was all right.

He couldn't get very close to the fire barrel because of the intense heat. He went around it and peered first into the barrel that had a lid on the end with three holes. It was empty. He turned toward the other one with a tattered mattress next to it and some kind of plastic cover, but there was no one inside that either.

He stayed there a few moments gazing in bewilderment at the empty habitation. Even though he'd been running a long time, his forehead had been dry until a moment ago. Now it was beaded in sweat from the fire that was roaring out of the one-third barrel. What did they burn, he wondered. And where did they go?

Completely puzzled, he turned toward the bridge.

∽ 13 ∾

THE YOUNG MAN COULDN'T immediately recognize what had happened. The lower part of the bridge looked different from before. It should have been dark-red, but now white was the prevailing color in keeping with the surrounding area. At first he thought that frost had made an enormous pattern, but the randomness of nature could not have made something so regular.

He was paralyzed by disbelief when he realized what he was looking at. He stared numbly at the long lines that densely followed one after the other all the way to the opposite bank. The white letters were too small for him to read, but it was unquestionably a written text. The manuscript appeared very neat. There were no corrections, everything was uniform, orderly. And above all enormous. The young man had no experience in such appraisals, but he wouldn't have been surprised if a voluminous book had been written under the bridge.

A whole host of puzzling questions plagued him.

Who had written this? And when? He'd run this way yesterday morning but hadn't noticed anything, and he certainly wouldn't have missed something as big as this. He hadn't noticed it right away today because his attention had been drawn to the flames that were still blazing behind him.

And then, how could such a huge job have been completed in just one day? And how had it been done, anyway? Complicated hanging scaffolding was needed to access the lower part of the bridge. And finally, what was written there? It certainly wasn't just graffiti.

Some of the answers could have been provided by the homeless who'd spent the previous day and night here, but they'd chosen this very moment to disappear. Maybe it wasn't by accident? Did their disappearance have something to do with this wonder? He looked around the habitation once more, hoping to catch sight of someone, but it was still empty.

The questions would have to remain unanswered for now. All but the one that concerned him.

What should he do?

He could pretend he hadn't seen anything and keep on running. But should he pass up a chance to be part of a happening like this? He was clearly the first one there because otherwise there would have been a crowd. And he might be able to profit from being first. If he made a name for himself, he might even earn something.

The natural thing would be to inform the police, but then there would be no benefit. He would be just an ordinary eyewitness. No, he'd rather call his journalist friend instead. He didn't have a high opinion of the tabloid where the man worked, but he still wouldn't mind being on the front page. And if he got a little something in addition for having informed them first. . . .

He reached into his pocket and then swore through clenched teeth. He hadn't brought his mobile phone. Fortunately he had a bit of change. The closest telephone booth was at the beginning of the bridge. He'd get there in a jiffy.

∽ 14 ∾

THE YOUNG MAN DIDN'T tell his friend why he was calling at the crack of dawn from the Red Bridge. Telephones were not trustworthy. He should just come, he wouldn't be sorry. The just-wakened journalist certainly didn't feel like going out into the black frost without a good reason. Was he going to miss an opportunity that might come along once in his career because of a little cold weather, asked the young man? He might become famous that very day. The prospect of fame was decisive. A quarter of an hour later his friend stopped his car next to the telephone booth at the beginning of the bridge.

The young man was still being secretive. He'd never been good with words and wouldn't know how to describe the wonder. Let the journalist be patient a bit longer. He would soon see it with his own eyes. As they descended the steps, the young man complained about being so disheveled from running. He wouldn't look nice on the front-page pictures. Maybe he'd be able to fix himself up a bit before the photojournalist got there. And then, as though remembering something, he hastened to add that he wasn't interested in fame, of course. He would be quite satisfied if they found some other way to show their gratitude for the service he'd rendered.

As soon as they got below the bridge, the young man realized that something was wrong. There wasn't any fire. Without a word of explanation, he ran toward the homeless' habitation. All he could see at the bottom of the fire barrel was a little pile of ashes. He crouched down and carefully put out his hand to the barrel, then touched the metal. It was ice-cold.

He stood up and turned toward the bridge. When his friend soon joined him, he was still standing there staring at the dark-red lower surface.

"Where's this wonder of yours?" asked his friend sullenly.

The young man didn't seem to hear him. He only replied when the question was repeated.

"It was here. . . ."

"Where here?"

He pointed along the bridge.

"Everything was covered in writing . . . white . . . to the other bank."

"I don't see a thing."

"It disappeared. . . ."

"How could it disappear?"

The young man shrugged his shoulders helplessly. "I don't know. . . ."

"Is this some sort of joke? You pulled me out of a warm bed this early because you felt like having a bit of fun?"

"No, I swear it's not that. You have to believe me. I saw it clearly, like I see you now. A huge manuscript . . . An entire book . . . And not only that." He motioned his head toward the fire barrel. "Fire was belching out of that. Almost up to the bridge. I couldn't get close because of the intense heat. . . ."

The journalist took a look at the cold ashes and then shook his head.

"Your picture will be on the front page but you don't have to fix yourself up. Disheveled like that you'll fit in perfectly with the copy I'm going to write."

THE JOURNALIST SIGHED, TURNED around and headed toward the steps.

 15

THE NEXT MORNING THE young man changed the route he ran. He no longer went under the bridge. First of all, it wasn't safe there because of the ice. Second, he didn't like coming across homeless people since he couldn't help them. Finally, wondrous hallucinations appeared there that seemed very convincing. Why would someone subject themselves to these problems for no reason? There was as much space for running as anyone could want.

Rumors about mysterious events under the Red Bridge periodically reached the tabloid's editors during the remaining winter months. On particularly cold nights the surface of the river apparently lit up as if someone had turned on a light under the bridge, although there wasn't one. Not only that, but a pattern similar to writing appeared on the water as though reflecting a gigantic manuscript from above. Since the Danube was always rippling, the text could not be read. This phenomenon was always accompanied by a roar, just as if the homeless had lighted a big fire on the bank, even though they were always short of firewood.

The editor-in-chief proposed that they check out the rumors, but a journalist explained there was no need. It was a hoax and he'd already fallen for it. Nothing unusual was going on around the Red Bridge. It was just idle jokers playing tricks on the gullible. Why should a self-respecting tabloid become one of their victims?

Fourth Wonder
White Bridge, Budapest

AN ELDERLY MAN IN a black coat, dark-yellow hat and red scarf stepped onto the White Bridge in Budapest on Sunday at 09:27.

He was not surprised to see there were no other pedestrians. Who but an oddball would go for a walk in such weather? He tilted his umbrella to protect himself from the icy rain slantin°g down, blown by the capricious wind. Cars were spraying water onto the pavement so he stayed by the railing to avoid being splashed. He had waterproof shoes but the bottoms of his pant legs were already wet.

Even though oddballs were not uncommon in his field, he didn't consider himself to be one. On the contrary, he was proud of the exemplary public image which befitted a reputable composer and conductor. Had he been able to go to the White Bridge at a more suitable time, he certainly would have done, both for social reasons and because he hadn't felt like leaving his hotel room in such rain and wind. But he'd had no choice.

His plane to Budapest yesterday afternoon had been

two hours late, so he'd gone straight to the concert hall from the airport. There had been barely enough time to get ready for the performance. As he conducted, he thought for a moment about taking a walk on the bridge after the concert, but when it was over fatigue got the better of him after the long, tiring day. Up until just a few years ago he'd still been full of vim and vigor, but after turning seventy-five he'd had to face the fact that old age was on his doorstep.

Although he valued his rest, he'd gotten up earlier than usual this morning to make up for what he'd missed yesterday. He had to leave for the airport at 11:45 and couldn't postpone his departure because he had another performance that evening in a different country. The tour had not initially included Budapest. His agent had been greatly surprised when he'd made a last minute request to organize a concert in the city on the Danube. He'd offered no explanation for this unexpected about-face. For years his agent had had to find pretexts to turn down invitations for the maestro to perform in Budapest without knowing why he disliked the city, and now suddenly he was the one who wanted to go there.

The old man had been crestfallen to see the weather change overnight. There'd been no need for an umbrella the night before and now he wondered if it would be enough. But he'd been determined to go even with a raging storm outside. This was his last chance to visit the White Bridge. He knew that he would never come to Budapest again. Neither as a conductor nor for a private visit.

The enthusiasm he brought to the concert podium hadn't faded, but that alone was not sufficient. Conducting was first and foremost demanding physical work. He was still able to do the job, but how would he feel in a year or two?

Then there was the doctor who warned him unremittingly not to tax his weakened heart. If the doctor had his way, there would be no more performances or long trips, let alone tours. He would also bristle to see him outside in such weather. If he wanted to live, said the doctor, it would be best to stay at home. He had no reason to complain. As a man with many talents, he would not have to give up much. Indeed, there would be no more conducting, but he could compose to his heart's content. And it was excellent therapy for heart disease. If only the doctor could prescribe it to everyone.

In addition to being disagreeable, the downpour made it hard for the old man to get his bearings. Holding the umbrella lowered in front of him blocked his view. He wondered whether he would be able to find what he was looking for even on a clement day. Nothing marked the three spots. They could only be distinguished in his aging memory, but could he rely on it?

Fifty-one years had passed since the last time he'd been there. Fortunately, the White Bridge looked exactly the same as it had half a century earlier. They must have renovated it recently; no traces of time could be seen. Bathed in sunlight and not drenched in rain, it would be glittering, matching its name. The way he remembered it.

The first spot should be the easiest to find. It was not far from the left-hand end of the downstream side of the bridge. But he couldn't say exactly where. He stopped after six or seven steps and stared at the railing. Thick arching chains connected the massive square pillars. Had it taken place between the first and second pillar or the second and third? He'd been certain this would become clear at first glance, but now he hesitated.

He would have stayed there longer, mulling things over, if he hadn't heard the rapid splashing of four paws on the wet pavement. The little black-and-white mongrel looked miserable: thin, mangy, drenched. Slobbering. Old. Its ears were cocked asymmetrically and its eyes were full of gum. The faded, worn-out red collar indicated that it had had an owner once.

It stopped for a moment in front of the composer and sniffed his pant leg cautiously. It wagged its tail, raised its head and gave a short bark as though wanting to say something. Its bark was hoarse and broken, resembling a rattle. The upcoming winter will be hard on it, thought the conductor. Maybe its last.

The dog continued along the bridge and the conductor turned back toward the railing. That's when he saw what he was looking for. The rain, wind and cars, the river's gray panorama through the railing, and the gloomy autumn day all suddenly disappeared and everything turned quiet. An enormous window in time seemed to open before him and he went back to that long-ago night in May. . . .

∽ 2 ∾

HE HAD JUST ARRIVED in Budapest. He knew only a few words of Hungarian, but they were enough to start studying composition. At the Conservatory, the universal language of music was mostly spoken. The joy of entering the prestigious school was only slightly dampened by the certainty that he would have a hard time learning the difficult language of the country where he would spend the next two years. It had nothing in common with his mother tongue, but this didn't trouble him. An obstacle is a challenge to a young person.

He'd been amazed by Budapest in many respects, but by the Danube above all because his hometown had no river. The magnificent bridges were like wonders of the world. He walked across them, mesmerized, whenever he had a chance. All were beautiful, but one soon became his favorite. Not a day went by without crossing the White Bridge at least once. He tried to do it in the evening when the lights bestowed a certain surrealistic air on the stone structure over the great river.

He'd reached the White Bridge later than usual that evening—twenty minutes to midnight. He was on his way back from a concert that had started at ten in a church in the other part of town that was renowned for its unique organs. Since public transport was hard to come by, he'd already walked a good half hour. A somewhat shorter walk awaited him from the bridge to his house. This was not a disheartening prospect since he was still under the influence of the concert and didn't feel like going to bed. The evening was mild, a breeze was rustling through the new leaves in the tops of the lindens and the smells of spring made his heart soar.

He was delighted to see that the White Bridge was empty. It was a rare privilege to have it all to himself. He felt like running with his arms wide open, but just as he started, he stopped dead in his tracks. He wasn't alone after all. There was a young woman just a dozen meters in front of him, but he'd overlooked her because she wasn't where one would expect. Her back turned, she was standing on the stone edge behind the thick chain connecting two pillars. She was bending forward, holding onto two massive links behind her back.

Hearing his rapid steps, she turned her head. She had short auburn hair, a thin face and large eyes. She started talking excitedly, evidently convinced that he was rushing to stop her from jumping. He didn't understand the words, but he did the tone. The voices of suicides are the same in all languages. If he got any closer she would let go of the links and plunge into the Danube.

He stood there without moving, feverishly considering what to do. Every idea that crossed his mind stumbled over the barrier of language. He could seek help from distant passers-by on the promenade along the river, but by the time he reached them and somehow explained what was going on, the young woman would probably have done what she intended.

The same would happen if he ran to a nearby telephone booth and called the police. He wouldn't be able to use gestures in that case and would have to rely on his broken Russian or English. But Budapest policemen, particularly on the night shift, were certainly not polyglots, something he'd seen for himself. They would most likely conclude that someone was playing a joke on them.

When he finally spoke, it was not the result of forethought. Panic struck him when the young woman turned her eyes back to the river. He had to do something. Words simply poured out of him. He realized that she wouldn't understand them, but hoped the tone would be sufficiently articulate.

He told her what one says to suicides: what she intended to do made no sense; the reasons compelling her to take her own life would seem unimportant the next day; she had her whole life ahead of her and had only just begun. And then he added something that isn't said to quite all suicides: it would be an immense, cosmic shame if she deprived the world of her beauty.

He stopped talking when she turned toward him once again. They stared at each other for a few moments and then a smile passed over her face. He replied in kind, proud of himself for turning a drawback into an advantage. Had he addressed her in Hungarian, she might not have replied this way. Understanding between them had been reached through complete lack of understanding. She was ashamed of committing suicide in front of a foreigner. He knew that nothing more needed to be said. It was enough to go toward her with outstretched arms.

 3

BUT HE DIDN'T.

He stood there rooted to the spot, eyes as big as saucers, open-mouthed, as a cascade of music washed over him. It swooped down on him from everywhere as though the bridge had suddenly turned into a gigantic orchestra. He was surrounded by countless invisible instruments creating a magical harmony. The trembling that overwhelmed him suppressed any rational questions. Later he would try to figure out what had happened. Now he had to surrender completely to the sound.

He should have had no trouble recognizing the composition, something this marvelous could not be unfamiliar, particularly for someone whose profession was music. A chill went down his spine when he soon realized why he couldn't guess the piece. How could he recognize something he'd never heard? That no one had ever heard? That was being heard for the first time now?

Still not moving, he gazed at the young woman. But the look she returned was bewildered, not mesmerized. Was it possible that she couldn't hear the music? That it was only accessible to him? She had to make an effort, she couldn't pass up this once-in-a-lifetime opportunity, something that might be the best reason to live.

As the tiny bit of awareness not engaged in listening pondered how to tell her this over the linguistic obstacle that separated them, she spoke. He realized this by her moving lips, because the music drowned out all other sounds on the bridge. He would not have understood even if he could have heard her, but the tone might once again hint at what she was saying. Now all he could rely on was the expression on her lovely face.

The young woman's bewilderment gave way to sadness when she fell silent, gazing at him mutely for a few moments. The last look in her large eyes would stay with him through the long decades that lay ahead. It was not accusing. It held only regret for the opportunity they had just missed. Then she turned toward the Danube graciously as though making a pirouette and spread her arms.

He longed with all his heart to shout and rush after her, but the crescendo that surged just then held him back completely. He uttered no sound and made not a move, his face crazily distorted by feelings that did not belong together. Tremendous rapture and unbearable pain flowed through him simultaneously. The spasm only worsened as he strove to hear her body fall into the water. But the inexorable music deprived him of this as well.

He remained at end of the bridge for a long time that night, although he didn't realize it until later. Listening to the compositions one after the other, he was unaware of the passage of time. Had anyone walked by, his rigid posture and crazy expression would have aroused suspicions, but there were no late passers-by and the passengers in cars drove by too quickly to notice anything unusual.

When the young woman was gone, he tried to fight the music. Although truly divine, it had caused her death. Tremendous willpower was needed to move his hands and put them firmly over his ears, but this had no effect. The sounds were still crystal clear, as though coming from inside his head.

He could do nothing to prevent it. He knew that pain would soon give way to rapture, he didn't want it but there was nothing he could do. When ecstasy had the upper hand, his only consolation was the thought that he was repaying her with his attentiveness. He was proud of his excellent memory for music. He would remember these notes well, write them down and dedicate them to her. They would be worthy of her beauty.

It was not until the early hours, when the cascade of music finally ran dry and he was heading home exhausted, that he realized it would not be simple to pay homage to the young woman. How could he publish the compositions? Whom would he identify as author? They would call him a lunatic if he explained their origin. He spent most of the way home thinking it over and finally realized he had no choice. If he wanted the world to hear them, he would have to sign them with his own name.

There was one more problem. He couldn't show the world everything he remembered from the bridge all at once, although the music certainly deserved it. Even one composition would arouse suspicions. A beginner certainly should not be able to create such perfect music. The best thing would be to add a few blemishes here and there and then fix them later.

And if he published them all right away, he would be expected to continue with no less talent and productivity. But that was impossible. Regardless of the explanation behind the miracle on the bridge, he had no reason to expect it would repeat itself, and he knew he would never be equal to such musical heights. So he would spread the publication of the compositions over several years. That would appear most natural.

He found out the young woman's name from the newspaper two days later. With the help of a dictionary, he read the report on her jump from the bridge when it appeared at the bottom of the page on tragedies. The case was barely worth mentioning in a country notorious for its number of suicides. Only five lines of text accompanied the small photograph. No one knew what had caused the nineteen-year-old flautist to take her own life. There had been no suicide note.

∽ 4 ∾

THE SOUND OF BARKING, muffled by the wind and rain, brought him back from the past. The mongrel had moved off some distance and was now looking at the opposite side, although no one was there. Clutching the umbrella handle more firmly, the old man continued down the bridge. The second place would be hardest to find. It was near the middle, but this time he could not expect any help from the railing. The late-summer incident had taken place on the pavement where nothing disturbed the uniformity.

In the days following the young woman's suicide he had continued to visit the White Bridge. He would reach the spot where she jumped into the Danube around a quarter to midnight and throw the flower he'd brought into the water. Then he would stand there a long time, riddled with guilt.

A dispassionate voice in his head softly reminded him that he hadn't let the flautist down, he'd desperately wanted to save her even if it meant losing the inimitable music, but it had impeded him entirely. His conscience, however, paid no attention to the whispers of common sense. Whenever they became louder, he would silence them with the memory of her last look and almost balletic movement toward the river before letting go of the links.

On his way back from the bridge the first few nights, he resented the music so much that he thought of tearing up what he'd started writing down and simply forgetting the rest. But when he picked up the notes, he faltered. How could he avenge one beauty by destroying another? Should he deprive the young woman of a lasting memorial and let her memory boil down to five lines in the newspaper?

He spoiled the first composition a bit and then took it to the Conservatory. After looking it over, his professor eyed him suspiciously and then took a pen and fixed what had been ruined. "Now it's better," he said, proverbially sparing with praise. Some of the great names in music received no more. "Bring something new when you have it."

The young man left his office all aglow. Only the most gifted students could hope for this. As he rushed to continue transcribing from memory, his conscience warned him that joy was out of place. The work was not his. It hadn't been difficult to smother that weak voice. He would have been committing an unforgivable sin if he'd stolen the composition from someone. But who could accuse him of theft in this case?

During his subsequent visits to the bridge, he started pricking up his ears. It was unconscious at first as he stood next to the railing after throwing the flower. The long hours would drag slowly by, at one point his thoughts would inevitably drift away from the young woman, there was nothing else to engage his mind but the sounds of the night.

The first time he caught himself trying to hear the bridge's music he was ashamed. It was like tarnishing the flautist's memory. If he were to be inundated again by the divine harmony for no special reason, her death would lose all meaning, although he could not explain what that meaning might be.

He'd dealt at length with what had happened that fateful night. The appearance of the music at the crucial moment had not seemed to be an accident, but whatever was behind this twist of fate eluded him. Why had the cascade thwarted him just as he'd almost saved her life? Was it a mere coincidence? In that case, the injustice was even greater.

Nevertheless, he kept listening intently, fooling himself that he was doing so against his will. He continued to go to the bridge around midnight, but not every day. Now he preferred to visit it during the daytime. Under the summer sun its immaculate whiteness was dazzling. He would prick up his ears as he walked across it, but the cacophony of the city was all he heard. And if the music were to appear, he reminded himself periodically, no attentive listening would be necessary. It would sweep over him fiercely, overpowering all other sounds.

At the end of July he went home for a month. It was the most productive summer vacation of his life. He took his memory full of music from Budapest and diligently started transcribing it. But pleasure was clouded by the frustration of not being able to publish everything right away. It was hard to restrain his youthful impatience. He consoled himself with the thought that before him lay at least a decade and a half as a very successful composer without arousing anyone's suspicions.

He returned to the city on the Danube at the end of the summer, wanting to meet his professor as soon as possible. And visit the White Bridge again.

THE DOG WAITED FOR the old man to catch up, then wagged its tail and continued down the bridge. The conductor raised his umbrella a little and looked at the upstream side to see what the mongrel had barked at. A new window in time opened the same moment.

 5

HE'D GONE STRAIGHT TO the Conservatory from the railway station. This time he hadn't spoiled the composition he'd chosen to show his professor. This was no longer necessary. Gifted students were expected to make progress. After reading the music, his professor gave him a probing look just as he had the first time.

"It seems you were inspired once again."

"Thank you," he replied with a smile.

"We'll play this at the fall concert."

He wanted to say how honored he was, but he still hadn't mastered enough Hungarian to say it properly so he just repeated, "Thank you," with a broader smile.

"Have you already conducted?"

"No."

"Composers conduct their works at the fall concert. You'll do all right. Composing is considerably harder than conducting. You can conduct even without inspiration. All you need is a little practice. So practice."

The student nodded his head and said, "Thank you," a third time, then turned to go. He was already at the office door when his professor spoke again.

"Have you given any thought to inspiration?"

"Not much."

"There is no greater mystery. What inspired you to compose this?"

The young man narrowed his eyes and shrugged his shoulders. "I don't know. It just came to me. . . ."

"It never comes without a reason." He paused and then mumbled a short sentence that the student didn't understand. The only word he thought he caught was "price." He waited for his professor to say something else, but his gaze had gone back to his desk.

The student left the Conservatory, went to his rented apartment and then out to dinner. Night was already far along when he reached the White Bridge. When he got there he realized he hadn't brought a flower. He sighed with regret. The florists were all closed. He could have gone to the nearby park and taken one surreptitiously, but after a moment's consideration decided not to. Somehow it didn't seem right.

Perhaps now was the time to stop bringing flowers whenever he went there. The bridge was not a cemetery after all. He still grieved over the young woman, of course, but grief could be expressed in other ways. He would always stop at the place where she had jumped and spend some time thinking about her. But there was no reason for the rest of the bridge to belong to grief and not joy.

Now as he walked, this very joy started to fill him. He had dreamed of moments such as this when he was away from Budapest: a wonderful evening in late summer on the prettiest bridge in the world. The thought of the fall concert not only as composer but also conductor turned the joy into euphoria. He felt like running. . . .

Just as he started to run, a dark-blue car coming his way slowed down and stopped at the curb in front of him. The young man stopped as well. He thought it was someone unfamiliar with Budapest who wanted to ask him a question. He smiled. What a person they'd found to ask. Indeed, he could get around the central part of town and already understood Hungarian rather well, but he still had trouble expressing himself.

He waited for someone to say something, but nothing happened. A good minute passed before the young man finally bent down and looked through the open window. The lighting on the bridge barely reached inside the car. In the gloom he saw the driver leaning forward, his head on the steering wheel. His face was turned the other way.

Just as the young man was about to ask if he needed help, the driver turned his head. The shock of recognition coincided with the smack of the cascade.

As music crashed on him from all around, he stared numbly at his professor's moving lips. Convulsions indicated how much effort was needed for every stammered word. Only something terribly important could be told that way. He made just as convulsive an effort to hear them, but the selfish music destroyed all other sounds. All he could do was lean over and watch, vainly resisting the ecstasy that had begun to wash over him.

Just as when the young woman was falling into the water, once again he felt his feelings split when the head sliding down the steering wheel coincided with the rising crescendo. Rapture collided head-on with excruciating pain. Even though he knew nothing would be achieved by it, he tried with might and main to move his hands.

This time, however, he could not raise them to his ears. His hands only reached the lower edge of the window. Realizing the trap he'd fallen into, he tried in despair to move them further, but could not. Seeing him in this position, passers-by and the passengers in cars would think he was chatting with the driver who had made a brief stop. No one would suspect the drama taking place before their eyes. No one would come to their assistance. It still might not be too late, but soon it would be for sure.

He spent almost two and a half hours by the car, powerless to turn his eyes away from his dead professor. Music inspired him relentlessly the whole time as he simultaneously adored and hated it. It filled his soul with heavenly grace and he did his utmost not to remember it, even though he knew it was senseless to resist. It carved itself in his memory like granite, making it impossible to forget.

He snapped out of the spell just as a car with flashing blue lights stopped behind his professor's car. It didn't take the patrol long to establish the facts. They were experienced policemen. The elderly driver had had a heart attack behind the wheel. That happened periodically. People should stop driving when they reached sixty. It was a good thing he hadn't lost control of the vehicle and had managed to stop at the curb. A few years ago on another Budapest bridge, an unlucky old driver's heart had also given out and he had broken through the railing and ended up in the Danube.

The patrol was accommodating toward the foreign student. They liked the fact that he spoke Hungarian, although with a strong accent. They checked his documents but did not take down his personal details. There was no need. It was not a violent death and the young man had been there by chance. The daze that had befallen him was understandable. He had certainly never seen a dead body before. After waiting for the ambulance and tow truck, they offered to give him a ride home, but he thanked them and said it would be easier to collect his wits if he walked.

∽ 6 ∾

HE WAS BROUGHT BACK to the present by a distant bark. The mongrel was standing some thirty meters from the end of the bridge, calling him. He headed toward it, thankful not to have to look for the third spot.

AS HE HAD WALKED home through the warm Budapest night, he'd sworn that he would never set foot on the White Bridge again. He wouldn't even go near it. He didn't want its gifts that came at such a terrible price.

As soon as he got home, he took a thick bundle of sheet music out of his still packed suitcase, the result of a month's diligent writing. He put all of his pent up anger into tearing it up, but this didn't ease his mind. The music was still embedded in the granite of his memory and nothing could dispel it.

He was surprised when he found out that his composition had been included in the fall concert program.

His professor had obviously managed to give it to the organizing committee after their last meeting in his office. He tried to get out of having it performed, saying he was dissatisfied with the work, but there was no backing out. The program had already been announced and his professor had given the composition high marks, which was an exceptionally rare event, so the student's dissatisfaction was disregarded. As a final point, the piece would have the privileged last place in the concert as the professor's final recommendation.

He climbed onto the podium determined to ruin the performance with bad conducting. Since he was inexperienced, no one would be able to criticize him for this. But the demonic music carried him away from the opening bars. Despite the fact that he had hardly practiced, he conducted as though in a trance, transmitting his fervor to the orchestra and then to the audience, filled mostly with professional musicians who were by no means easy to charm.

Stirred by the applause that seemed never to end, the Conservatory's administration soon proposed that the young composer be the star of the winter concert. The second half of the program would be all his. He would have a chance to conduct four of his compositions. Only the Conservatory's most outstanding students were given such an honor.

Swayed by his first successful performance, he nevertheless tried to find a way out. He said he didn't have enough time to write four compositions by the middle of December. He would try but couldn't promise anything. The chances of him succeeding were not very great.

He resisted temptation until the very last moment. He realized that submitting the compositions would be an inexcusable betrayal not only of the young woman and of his professor but of himself as well, but the thunderous applause kept ringing in his ears. The night before the deadline, when he set about transcribing the music from the granite slabs of his memory, he tried to convince himself that this was only an exception that would never be repeated, that he was doing it solely to pay homage to those who had been sacrificed for his sake. But this did nothing to decrease the sinking feeling with which he copied down the notes.

He spent most of the time until the concert transcribing. First he recopied what he'd torn up in anger and then what he'd heard in his dead professor's company. He had somehow to redeem himself for this new weakness. All he managed to come up with was that since he couldn't forget the music he'd heard twice on the White Bridge, it made no difference whether it existed in music manuscript books as well.

When he was finished, he calculated that he had enough compositions for three decades and maybe even more if he published them at moderate intervals. But this calculation was made just out of curiosity. He was certainly not going to publish anything else.

When he received a telegram from home, he was filled with both happiness and dread. In spite of half the continent being snow-swept, his parents were coming to the winter concert. How could they miss their son's first great success?

HE PATTED THE MONGREL when he got to it, then lowered his umbrella and raised his head toward the leaden sky. Rain fell on his face for just a moment and then he was showered by large snowflakes from the third window in time.

SNOW WAS A RARITY in the south where he originated. Even when it fell it wouldn't stay long, barely covering the streets and roofs. It was hard for him to imagine his hometown buried in snowdrifts. He didn't have to imagine anything here. After a three-day snowstorm, Budapest seemed to disappear under a white blanket more than a meter deep in some places.

The surreal impression was increased by the sight of skiers taking over the unplowed pavement. Only a few of the main streets and two bridges were plowed. Life seemed suspended. The Conservatory administration thought about canceling the winter concert, but since this would mean breaking a long and illustrious tradition, they decided to hold it nonetheless.

His parents' arrival could not have come at a worse time. Their train was frequently held up and had been slowly making its way towards Hungary for almost two days. The approaches to Budapest would be the most difficult. Although the railroad workers were doing their best, the tracks were mostly snow-swept.

Early on the afternoon of the concert, he was relieved to hear finally that their train was expected in about an hour and a half. He promptly got ready to go to the train station. It would have taken him ten minutes by public transport, but he couldn't count on that now. Under normal circumstances, he could get there in three-quarters of an hour on foot, but the snow would certainly slow him down. If only he knew how to ski. . . .

Indeed, this would not have been much use on the way back from the station. He would have had to carry his parents' luggage and help them as well. They were no more skilled than he was at getting about in the snow and they would be exhausted after the long and difficult trip. He wondered whether he would have any time to rest after they got settled. The concert started at six and another hour's walk awaited them from their hotel to the Conservatory.

Had he been able to imagine such a snowstorm in Budapest, he would have found a closer hotel. Actually, when he gave it some thought, the best thing would have been for his parents not to come. He was happy they were there, of course, but even though the concert was important, it was not worth so much effort. They would have other opportunities to attend his performances. He was just at the beginning of his career, after all.

As soon as he entered the swirling snowflakes in front of his house, he had to make a choice that hadn't occurred to him. Which way should he go? The White Bridge was one of the two in service. He had sworn that he would never cross it again, but the other bridge was on the opposite side of the city. There was no telling how long it would take him to walk to the train station if he headed in that direction. Not to mention the return trip with his parents. Should he expose them to a long and unnecessary detour just because of his misconception?

During the long hours of transcribing the compositions from memory, the thought that what had happened to him on the White Bridge had been just a coincidence had slowly taken root in his consciousness. It had been very tempting to conclude that the bridge's demonic effect was behind the whole thing. At first glance, two deaths right when he was engulfed by inspiration could not be accidental. There was a simpler explanation, however. Not a very probable one, but it was natural.

The young woman would have killed herself for whatever reason even if he hadn't appeared, and his professor—as he'd learned in the meantime—had suffered for years from heart disease. He survived two heart attacks, but not the third. The young man's presence had nothing to do with the two deaths. He simply happened to be on the bridge at a fateful hour for both of them. This coincidence would ring hollow in literature, but life sometimes organizes unbelievable twists of fate.

This realization had brought him respite. Above all, it relieved his conscience of the terrible burden of guilt that troubled him, even though he could not clearly pinpoint what it was. In addition, he no longer had to repudiate the music as something that did not belong to him. It was his and he had no reason not to embrace it. Or the fame that awaited him.

If there was anything mysterious on the bridge, all it concerned was inspiration. Why did it only come to him there? After lengthy consideration, he could find no answer. This had not been hard to take. Hadn't it been the professor who said there is no greater mystery?

He'd acted rashly when he'd decided not to go there anymore. It was like cutting off the wings that were carrying him to the highest pinnacles of music. He should have done the opposite and taken that crossing over the Danube as often as possible—for the sake of new compositions and to dispel his doubts once and for all. When the cascade washed over him the next time, no one's death would go along with it. That's how it had to be. Two coincidences were more than enough.

He trudged through the deep snow toward the White Bridge.

When he got there he was sweaty and out of breath. His parents would have a very hard time walking through the snowbound streets of Budapest. A sight frequently seen along the way made him think of buying a sled and proposing that he pull his mother and father with their luggage to the hotel and then to the Conservatory. That would make it easier for them all. His father might agree, but his mother certainly would not. She would find riding on a sled undignified and would rather struggle through the snowdrifts.

As he approached the Danube, it seemed as though an enormous odd-shaped cake with a thick layer of whipped cream stretched across the river. Wrapped in a snowy blanket, the bridge was perfectly attuned to its name. Everything on it was white. Even though a snowplow cleared the pavement every fifteen minutes or so, a new layer of snow would start to form as soon as it passed.

When the young man was quite close to the bridge, the lights went on. Although afternoon was not far along, an early dusk had started to fall. The snow caused him a lot of trouble but also filled him with excitement. He saw that same blend of misery and joy on the ruddy faces of the people he encountered along the way. The orangey glow that spread all around subdued the former and enhanced the latter. This was facilitated by the fact that there were no other pedestrians on the bridge and vehicles rarely passed.

Euphoria, welling up inside him, announced a new cascade. It washed over him after barely thirty meters. The small part of his soul not encompassed by the music was filled with twofold sensations. Satisfaction at having his hopes come true greatly prevailed. There was no longer any doubt: he didn't have to pay for inspiration with someone's death. It had come without any price, which was all that made sense. Just like the other two times, except then the unbelievable coincidence had clouded his perception.

His concern that he would now stay on the bridge rather longer only slightly diminished his happiness. Thankfully he had left early. Then again, the train would probably not arrive at the newly expected time. And if he didn't make it in time to meet his parents on the platform, it wouldn't be the end of the world. He could justify his delay by the extremely bad weather in Budapest. In any case, what was a little waiting for their son at the train station compared to the gift he was now receiving? And who else could he expect to understand if not his parents, even though he, of course, could not confide in them?

As though wanting to repay him for his previous suffering, the music was merciful. The cascade lasted less than an hour, but it was no less sumptuous. The same number of compositions as before were chiseled into the granite of his memory, as though coming at an accelerated pace. Unless he let impatience get the better of him, he had before him almost half a century of steady, productive life as a composer. And if the bridge continued with its generosity, he could even publish more often.

In the throes of delight, he laughed out loud when the rapture ended and he saw how much snow had fallen on him in an hour. It had almost buried him. He'd merged with the bridge. Had anyone passed by, they certainly would have wondered why he was standing motionless in the snowstorm, but luckily no one had. Those passing by slowly in a car would think that someone had made a snowman on the sidewalk.

He briskly brushed off the snow and continued toward the train station, trying to run through the drifts.

He was heartened to see a crowd of people in front of the entrance. That could mean either the train had not yet arrived or had just pulled in. In any case, he wouldn't be late. But as soon as he entered the large station building, he realized that something was wrong. It was full of people, but the usual clamor had been replaced by silence, broken here and there by sobbing.

His insufficient knowledge of Hungarian had never been a greater problem. It took some time to find out what had happened—first from bits of conversation around him that he managed to understand and then from the information counter when he finally reached it through the large crowd.

When the train was quite close to Budapest, it had come across the last big snowdrift. The engineer's patience had worn thin. Instead of waiting for the track workers to remove the obstacle, he had rushed into it headlong, counting on the locomotive's great power. But he had overestimated; the locomotive did not break through it and overturned. This might not have been so terrible had the track not run right next to the Danube at that spot. The locomotive had pulled the first two cars along with it into the icy river.

The fate of the passengers in these cars was still uncertain. People anxiously awaited new information at the station, hoping that those they'd come to pick up were in the other cars or by some miracle had survived the fall into the Danube.

The young man did not join them. Walking in a daze, he made his way through the crowd in the station building and went out into the still swirling snow. He had no reason to stay inside and wait for the news.

Unlike the others, he had no hopes. He knew that his parents had been in one of the first two cars and that they had not survived the icy river. Just as he knew beyond reasonable doubt what had led to this outcome.

He stood in front of the station for a long time, slowly being wrapped in white again. He wanted nothing better than to go back inside, buy a ticket and take the first train to anywhere. Just as far away from Budapest as possible. But tonight no train would either reach the city or leave it. The trains might be interrupted for days until the storm finally passed and the tracks were repaired.

He finally left and took the roundabout way to the Conservatory. He almost ran over the other bridge in service, hands firmly pressed over his ears. He spent the time until the concert apart from his colleagues, who saw nothing unusual in that. Excited young musicians often sought seclusion before a concert.

He did not get spruced up for the podium. He went out disheveled with his hair still wet. This would not have been allowed had he been only the conductor, but they were lenient toward exceptional composers. They alone had the right to be a bit extravagant.

He started conducting like a madman. Twice the performance was almost interrupted because the orchestra could not keep up with him. But as the music gained momentum, it seemed to have an effect on him. He pulled himself together and got in step with the musicians. Soon the orchestra was under an enchanted spell that quickly spread to the audience.

The first three compositions received loud applause and the fourth was followed by an ovation. Everyone in the auditorium was on their feet. But the composer and conductor quickly left the stage without taking a bow. He was expected to come out again, but he didn't.

When the applause finally turned to confusion among the audience, they went looking for him. The doorman told them that he had rushed out of the Conservatory without his coat. No one saw him again. Three days later, as soon as the snowstorm passed and the trains were running, he left Budapest in a fever, firmly resolved never to return.

8

AFTER THE THIRD TIME window closed, the old man took out a large black silk handkerchief and wiped his dripping face. Then he looked around the bridge. He wasn't surprised to see that the dog had disappeared. It was gone because there was nothing else to show him. The White Bridge had dismissed the guide it had kindly provided, helping him to find all three spots he'd wished to visit from his past.

But he had not returned to this city after more than half a century just because of the past, despite swearing he would never go back. He didn't feel like a criminal returning to the scene of the crime. He'd made peace with his conscience long ago when, in spite of everything, he hadn't renounced his career as a composer and conductor.

Notwithstanding the difficult time he'd been through, in the beginning and later, now he was convinced that he'd done the right thing. Had he not, the world would have been a poorer place without this exceptional music and his behavior toward the four dead people would have been no better. On the contrary, only the music gave their sacrifice any meaning. Otherwise it would have been in vain. Had he agreed with this sacrifice in advance, the blame would be his, of course, but he was never asked. He was never given a choice. He had always been presented with a *fait accompli.*

One dilemma he had nonetheless never been able to resolve, even though he'd thought about it all through the years. Why had divine inspiration come at such a terribly high price? Wouldn't the world be a much nicer and more righteous place if he'd received it without any toll? Could music, even if it was perfect, be enough to redeem an imperfect world?

Another unanswered question was whether he'd been an exception, or whether other great musicians had paid a similar price. There had been only rare and unreliable intimations about it in the many autobiographies he'd read. Indeed, he'd expected nothing less. Who would have reason to leave a trace of the dark side of their inspiration? He would keep his a secret too.

He could not return to Budapest without confronting his past, but it was concern for the future that had brought him back. His long-ago calculation had proven accurate. The compositions chiseled in granite had lasted around half a century. He had nothing left to transcribe from his memory. That in itself was not terrible. His opus was one that would have been the envy of any composer, both for its quantity and its quality. He could even stop composing altogether.

He could have resigned himself to this fact—he knew that the supply was relentlessly decreasing—had the doctor not prohibited him from conducting at the same time. Suddenly he faced the danger of being left without any active musical life and this would be very hard on him. The doctor had nothing against composing, however. He had actually even recommended it as excellent therapy for an ailing heart. But since he hadn't a clue about the composer's secret, he had no way of knowing that the therapy he recommended was unavailable to his patient.

Bewildering his agent, he had come to the city on the Danube in the hope that the bridge would bestow music on him once again, thereby prolonging both his composing career and his life. He did not doubt that the new gift would also require payment and was ready for it.

He couldn't imagine, though, who would be sacrificed this time. He'd come to the realization that the previous victims were not chosen at random. There was a rising scale of intimacy from the unknown young woman to his professor and then his parents. But who was closer to him than his mother and father? That would be his children, but he had no children. He was actually not closely attached to anyone. This fact had finally settled the matter. The bridge could not take a greater sacrifice from him than the previous ones. He would somehow be able to bear a smaller one.

He looked around again, standing on the spot where he'd been almost buried in snow some fifty years ago. The temperature must have dropped a little. Snowflakes started falling with the rain, turning it to sleet. What now, he wondered. He had almost reached the far bank and the bridge had only opened windows to the past for him. There was no sign of the future.

He turned with a sigh and headed back. There was no sense waiting in such bad weather. He didn't have the time, either. A day full of obligations awaited him. He finally had to reconcile himself to the fact that the bridge refused to give him another present. He'd feared such an outcome, but now it seemed no more than fitting.

He had no right to expect mercy. The bridge had

never been kindly disposed to him: it gave but it also took. The price of its gifts went up every time. But the old man had no greater sacrifice to give in return. It was foolish to hope that he could get something without price. He should have realized it before. Returning to Budapest had been a mistake.

He would follow the doctor's advice and not go on tour again. He would stop conducting for good. He would miss the concert podium, the ovations that greeted him and sent him off, but one could live without them, presumably. Just as there were other therapies for a weak heart besides composing.

These thoughts brought him relief. He continued more briskly toward the middle of the bridge as though a burden had suddenly been lifted off his shoulders. How strange it was that simple solutions sometimes appear seemingly out of nowhere. Euphoria he'd not felt in a long time filled his heart.

The same instant he knew what was about to happen, even though more than fifty years separated him from the previous three times. Euphoria on the bridge had always heralded the cascade.

Over the years he had often tried to relive the memory of the first time it had hit him. He'd seemed to succeed periodically, but now he realized he'd been nowhere close. A faded memory was no match for an orgasm of music.

Before he surrendered to it, he had just enough time to smile at the pointlessness of his umbrella. It could protect him from the strongest downpour, but was completely useless under the ferocious cascade. He let it go and laid himself open completely to the elements. The wind picked up the open umbrella and swept it over the railing in an instant.

He had no idea what he'd done to deserve the bridge's mercy, but that was irrelevant now. He would mull it over later after the music fell silent. Just as he would start making plans for a new life. There would be no more worrying about his heart because it would be protected by the best therapy, and with a stronger heart he might be able to go back to conducting and touring. If the doctor was still against it, he would simply find another one. This one's excessive caution irritated him.

But all of that could wait. Nothing was more important right now than the music he was finally receiving without a sacrifice in return. He gave himself over completely to listening.

Already deep in the throes of ecstasy, the realization that something was wrong broke through from the edge of his awareness. The music was passing through him without leaving any trace. There were no blank granite slabs in his memory on which to engrave it. Everything he'd heard was disappearing forever.

Panic filled him. He had to do something, he couldn't let this last and most important gift from the bridge evaporate into thin air, but he was unable to move. And even if he could, what would he do? Where could he get hold of blank slabs?

He knew he was not supposed to get excited; the doctor regularly warned him that it could be fatal for his heart. That's why he always carried medicine with him. He had it now in the inside pocket of his jacket, but since he was unable to move, it might as well have been in his hotel. If only there was some way he could get hold of it. . . .

He started to raise his hand slowly as bliss and despair alternated on his face. When he touched the plastic vial, he was sweating so much it was as though rain had fallen underneath his clothes too. It seemed to take forever to unscrew the cap. Finally it came off, but this was only half the job.

He wasn't sure whether a pill had shaken into his hand. It took a long time to pull his clenched fist through the opening in his coat. The agony of waiting for his fist to open was quickly alleviated by the sight of two blue lozenges. He had to close his hand again so the rain didn't melt the pills on the way to his mouth.

As his hand got closer, a new instrument suddenly appeared, overpowering all the others. Instead of pouring down from above, it seemed to come from his ears. He didn't recognize it. Sounding like a primitive drum, it beat out a simple, accelerating rhythm.

He frowned. What was this intrusion? Why was it spoiling the divine music? He thought he could dispel it by shaking his head. But he didn't have the strength for such an effort. Perhaps he would if he swallowed the pills.

When his hand was just below his chin, the music was almost hushed. He had to strain to make it out in the background. And then when the drumming started its final ascent, no straining was enough. There was no room for other sounds along with this irrepressible rise.

In the meantime, snow had overpowered the rain and was coming down hard, creating a thickening curtain around him. Two climaxes merged into one. The crescendo of drumming seemed to burst in his head as the swirling snow draped him completely.

When a moment later he started to fall through the infinite silence and whiteness, he felt disembodied and light, as though hanging in the air.

Fifth Wonder
Blue Bridge, Novi Sad

A BIRD-DOG GOT ONTO the Blue Bridge in Novi Sad on Sunday at 23.13. Someone unapprised might have thought that the dog didn't realize where he was. It's easy to lose one's way in the pitch dark. The bridge lights and streetlights weren't on, not a single façade window was alight, the neon signs were off and the entire city had been swallowed up by the moonless night.

In spite of the obscurity, if someone had nonetheless noticed the dog and if that person had had a compassionate heart, they certainly would have chased him off the bridge. That was the last place to be this night. Not even the surrounding area was safe. The residents of the houses along the Danube had withdrawn to basement shelters or sought more distant safe havens.

But no one was in the vicinity when the dog came out onto the Blue Bridge. And even if someone had been there, they would have been wrong to chase him away for altruistic reasons. He wasn't there by accident and no danger threatened him. On the contrary, the bridge was waiting for him, ready to protect him.

Indeed, it would have been better if the dog had gotten there earlier and not at the last minute. Well, that's how it is with bird-dogs, thought the Blue Bridge with an inaudible sigh. They have lots of good qualities, but are proverbially unreliable when it comes to timekeeping. What's most important, however, is that he's finally here. Now we can take off. It's high time.

Once the dog had scampered to the middle, the bridge went into action. It was a real shame that owing to the circumstances there were no eye-witnesses. What happened next was a rare sight. The bridge easily broke its connections to both banks and the two massive towers in the river, as though they were tied together with paper ribbons. As it rose, it seemed to be made not of tons of metal but of some downy substance almost untouched by gravity.

It went straight up without a sound, like a balloon. The bird-dog stuck his head through the railing and stared at the darkness below. What a view it would be if the city weren't in the middle of a blackout, he thought wistfully. He'd always envied the birds he hunted. The world must look wondrous from the air. Now he was finally soaring and all he could see down below was solid darkness. It just wasn't fair.

They'd been rising for around ten minutes when something began to glimmer, not on the ground, however, but in front of them, like a swarm of fireflies in formation rapidly approaching from the west. The dog gazed at them curiously, then looked questioningly at the bridge that continued its ascent undisturbed.

In the glow of the fire gushing out of their tails, when the fireflies were quite close the bird-dog discerned that they were actually enormous birds. He knew all about feathered creatures, of course, that was his profession, but he had yet to see any like this. They had unusually stiff wings they didn't flap. He backed away from the railing when the birds roared over his head; shortly after they had passed there was a terrible clap of thunder. They took no notice of the bridge, as though it didn't interest them or they couldn't see it in the dark.

The bird-dog ran to the other railing. Along with the blazing tails, tiny explosions now began to punctuate the darkness, like someone down there had set off fireworks in honor of the large flock. But this was happening much lower down, as though the firework rockets were not powerful enough to reach the elevation where the birds were flying.

Suddenly three simultaneous explosions flashed at almost the same place on the ground. They had a tremendous impact even on the high-flying bridge. In the fleeting burst the dog recognized where they'd exploded. Three geysers were spouting out of the Danube on the spot they had just left.

Puzzled, the dog showered the bridge with questions. The answers he was given were reassuring. Yes, the birds had flown in to harm the Blue Bridge, but the whole thing had been very naive. As though Danube bridges could come to any harm. Not even time could touch them, let alone birds. No, the bridge would not punish the birds for wanting to hurt it. The bridge neither punished nor bore a grudge. No, they would not go back to Novi Sad as soon as the birds left. They were not soaring into the air to get away from the birds but because an important undertaking awaited them.

 2

RUSHING BACK TO THE west, the birds roared over the Blue Bridge. Despite the fact that everything had been duly explained to him, the dog could not resist the challenge. Front paws set upon the railing, he barked until the last firefly went out in the distance. The bridge sighed a second time. How could bird-dogs be brought to their senses when they thought with their instincts and hearts and not with their heads?

Not long afterward, lighted lines and grids started crisscrossing the darkness beneath the bridge. Since the dog was unused to heights, particularly at night, he didn't understand what was going on. He gazed at the archipelago of flickering islands in fascination. They appeared to be just below the railing. If he jumped over it, he would land on them.

Fortunately, the bridge was keeping careful watch of the bird-dog. It knew quite well who it was dealing with: the most reckless, impressionable and impetuous species of dog. Things would be no better during the day. Then he would probably realize how high they were, but would get it into his head that he could fly. Bird-dogs are also very vain. How could they let birds outdo them at anything? A third sigh was inevitable.

The dog stayed by the railing until they had almost fully descended and vertigo engulfed him when they were already quite low. The lighted geometric patterns turned into crisscrossing rows of streetlights. A town stretched out beneath them. The bridge had told him it would be some time before the return to Novi Sad and since he didn't know any other town, he assumed at first that the bridge had changed its mind.

But the bird-dog had virtues along with his faults. Sometimes, for example, he was quick-witted, and he was good at distinguishing shades of color. The streetlights in Novi Sad were not quite like this. His fear

gave way to excitement when he realized he was in another town. He went back to the railing inquisitively.

Now they were gliding above a large river. The re-
flection of the lights along its banks shimmered on the
dark surface of the water. This must be the Danube,
concluded the dog. Indeed, this was not particularly
insightful. He might have thought of another river, but
he knew of no other than the Danube. He was generally poor in geography.

Where were they? Before he could ask the bridge,
another bridge started to come into view under them,
drawing his attention. It was sturdier than the Blue
Bridge, made of massive stone with an orange film
drawn over its whiteness. When the White Bridge was
in full view, the Blue Bridge slowly made its final de-
scent next to it. Even though the bird-dog was very
sensitive to physical disturbances, he didn't feel it when
they stopped.

Nothing happened for a few moments. And then in
the middle of the Blue Bridge a small part of the railing
moved aside like a sliding door. Right afterward the
same thing happened on the White Bridge. The bird-
dog froze as though stalking a bird and stared fixedly
at the passage between the two bridges.

The first to come through was a young woman with
short auburn hair, a thin face and large eyes. The late
middle-aged man who followed looked to the bird-dog
like a professor. He would have had trouble explaining
where he got such an impression, but luckily no one
asked for one. A couple that looked like they'd spent
most of their long lives together was the next to cross
over to the Blue Bridge. They were carrying two large
suitcases that were more cumbersome than heavy.

Next came an elderly gentleman in a black coat,

dark-yellow hat and red shawl, carrying a large umbrella even though the night was clear. He was followed by a young man with tousled hair. The bird-dog's experienced eye immediately noted a certain similarity between the last two newcomers. They seemed to be related, perhaps father and son. That's how the son will look when he reaches his father's age, he thought.

Just when it seemed that the transfer to the Blue Bridge was finished, someone else arrived. The bird-dog's hackles rose instinctively, but relaxed as soon as he got a better look at the mongrel. No danger threatened from the thin, mangy dog with a slobbering snout, particularly since it took no notice of him. It joined the people who were standing around the two suitcases.

Since the bird-dog's view was partially blocked, he couldn't properly make out what was happening over there. The suitcases were opened and they all took something out of them. He saw what it was when the musicians moved apart, each one holding their instrument. The young woman had a flute, the professor a violin, the married couple two oboes, the older gentleman a viola and the young man a piccolo.

That's half an orchestra, thought the bird-dog. All they're missing is a conductor. But the conductor was there too. The mongrel jumped onto the railing holding a baton in its teeth. The bird-dog eyed it in disbelief. Was the orchestra going to be led by a mutt with uneven ears? One of them at least must be deaf. And they had counted him out, even though he was renowned for his discriminating hearing. The world wasn't fair, he concluded sadly once again.

The conductor tapped the baton on the railing twice. The musicians raised their instruments and lights blazed on the Blue Bridge the same instant. But the music did not ring out. They all just stood there without moving. What are they waiting for, wondered the bird-dog in bewilderment. The answer came from the railing. First one sliding door closed and then the other. At first the White Bridge seemed to be sinking, but it was just an illusion. They took off as imperceptibly as they had landed.

The Blue Bridge was high above Budapest when the orchestra finally started to play.

3

THE BIRD-DOG READILY LISTENED to music whenever he had a chance. One might think such chances were few and far between, but that would be wrong. The dog was not exactly allowed into concert halls, but there was music in other places if you had a sharp ear. And not even that was necessary if your path took you in the vicinity of a roadside tavern where the rafters rang with the sound of musicians out of sync, a shrieking songstress and whooping patrons.

The bird-dog naturally stayed away from such dives. What he heard there was an insult to his ear. But on nice days he gladly stopped under an open window where captivating music streamed out of a radio or some other device. Then he would turn all ears. He took no notice of birds at such times. One could fly right under his nose and even land in front of him, and he would be totally disinterested.

Before the orchestra started playing on the Blue Bridge, the dog had been filled with dread. The musicians didn't exactly inspire confidence. They seemed mismatched, like a pick-up band. But the first bars dispelled all his doubts. He had never heard anything so enchanting. He bristled with excitement.

Sometimes he suppressed his instincts when he listened to music or a pleasing birdsong washed over him. Instead of striking down the songbird, he would lie back and enjoy the moment. The warble would seem to come from the sky. Now, however, he was in the sky and he was the only listener. Could the best concert hall compare with this? What more suitable place to listen to heavenly music than in the sky?

Filled with delight, he had to give credit to the conductor. He'd been wrong about the mongrel. It had seemed the least capable of making music of them all. Appearances, however, had been highly deceiving. Even without the help of its front paws, the mutt was doing a compelling job of conducting the orchestra. The baton in its teeth unerringly wove the sounds of the instruments into a single strand. Not even the bird-dog could have done a better job.

Intoxicated by the music, he closed his eyes. The flickering grids of distant towns moved under the bridge again, but for the dog they had lost their initial charm. In any case, they were now dimmed by the bridge's lights. Eyes closed, listening was all that mattered.

He opened his eyes when the music stopped, but had no time to express his delight. He'd been certain they were still way up high, but once again they'd landed next to a Danube bridge. This one was red and the lights on it were white, not orange. Where are we now, he wondered. The bridge whispered the name of the town, but it didn't mean much to him. He would have to learn a bit about geography, he decided in embarrassment. If he'd known such a trip was imminent, he would have done it, of course, but who could have guessed . . . ?

The conductor jumped off the railing and the musicians started packing up their instruments. After this was done, the couple sat on the suitcases, the mongrel settled in between them and the others gathered behind. The bird-dog timidly joined the group so he wouldn't be the only one to stand aside. He stood at the end next to the young woman. He was filled with pride when the flautist patted his head. He wagged his tail briskly to thank her for her excellent playing.

The small talk stopped when the sliding doors started to open again. When two men appeared they were met by thunderous applause. The bird-dog was in a quandary, but tried not to show it. What have these two tattered fellows done to deserve such a warm welcome? It must be the books, what else? Each one was carrying three thick volumes.

When they got on to the Blue Bridge, they bowed and then approached the spot from which the mongrel had conducted. They put the books on the pavement and sat down on them, leaning their backs against the railing. The bird-dog was astonished. How could they abuse books like that? Even illiterate dogs would treat them with greater respect. How strange that the musicians didn't reprimand the two of them. They were still looking at them admiringly.

The larger ragamuffin then took a creature out from under his old army coat and set it on the railing. The bird-dog didn't recognize it at first because he'd never seen a member of his species that was almost hairless. Like it's been stripped, he thought in disgust. But was a better dog to be expected, living among the homeless? And what did they intend to do with it? It must help them with their begging, doing some sort of act. Could that be the reason for the applause? There was still time to change his mind about the musicians.

When the smaller ragamuffin, wearing thick glasses, also stuck his hand into the opening of his threadbare coat, the bird-dog winced. This one wasn't going to take out a freak too, was he? He sighed with relief when a worn-out folder was pulled out. Was that something they used in their act? The new applause additionally confused him.

The man smiled in gratitude and then opened the folder. It contained a fairly large number of handwritten pages. He handed the first one to the bigger ragamuffin who raised it in front of the little dog. The musicians stopped moving around.

The act did not start at once, however. The bird-dog already had enough experience to know what came before it. The sliding doors closed and the Red Bridge seemed to sink. When the Blue Bridge was far enough above Bratislava, the time had come for their performance.

$\backsim$ 4 $\backsim$

THE BIRD-DOG COULDN'T BELIEVE his ears. If he'd tried to guess what was about to happen, he never would have expected this. The tiny monstrosity that would have turned the stomach of any self-respecting dog started to read. Indeed, in a thin voice—a more masculine one did not go with its size—but a very articulate and flowing one. The diction was impeccable, like that of a first-rate announcer or actor.

Twofold feelings came over the bird-dog. He was proud, of course. Even though many people had doubts about dogs, he had not lost confidence in his species. He believed that they were capable of a variety of accomplishments, although, to be honest, he'd never thought they would embrace reading. On the other hand, he felt this was once more unfair. Of all dogs, why had one as nondescript as this mastered the skill? It would be far more elegant if he were the one reading on the railing, if only he knew how.

What he heard made it clear that it was reading and not merely pretending to read. People unaccustomed to dog language might have been deceived by the squeaky barking, everything sounded the same to them, but the two dogs in the audience could not be fooled. The bird-dog glanced at the mongrel. It looked happy, although not surprised, as though knowing what was up.

The reading sounded perfect and the text itself was excellent. The bird-dog was enchanted after the very first page of the manuscript in the green folder. What exciting material, what style, what expression. If his literary experience were more abundant, he might have noted some flaw, but he was happy to know quite little about prose. Sometimes too much knowledge hinders more than it helps.

The first page was read in a jiffy. It took much less time than if a human had read it. And no wonder, thought the bird-dog with a new wave of pride. It's a well-known fact that dogs' vocal abilities greatly surpass those of humans. See, we can read but do they know how to bark? If the hairless thing continued at this speed, it would have read the whole thick manuscript before they reached their new destination.

The bigger homeless man gave the first page back to the smaller one and received the second one in return. But the page that had been read did not end up in the folder at the bottom of the pile, as one would expect. Holding it in front of him, the writer briefly rummaged through the patched pocket of his coat, took out a lighter, set fire to the edge of the paper, waited for the flame to engulf it and then threw it over the railing.

What barbarism, thought the horrified bird-dog. Is that the way to treat a manuscript? It might be the only copy. Not even the author has the right to destroy it. Such magnificence no longer belongs to him alone. Don't the others realize it? Why don't they stop him? Nothing of the kind was attempted and there was even more applause when the burning sheet disappeared under the railing of the bridge.

The bird-dog moved away from the young woman. He didn't want to be associated with those who treated literature in that way. What he really wanted to do was leave the bridge in protest, but this was impossible, unfortunately. When a new sheet was soon placed in front of the little dog, the bird-dog decided to close his eyes again. He would not open them until the reading was over. That way he would enjoy it more fully and not have to watch the read-out sheets being burned.

The only thing that disturbed his enjoyment was the applause at regular intervals. The bird-dog would shake his head angrily every time, closing his eyes even more tightly. He hesitated to open them when the manuscript had been read to the end. The final applause was thunderous and never-ending. The barbarians must be greeting the burning of the last sheet instead of rewarding the little dog for its wonderful performance.

Since he couldn't keep his eyes closed forever, he squinted through them. A number of surprises awaited him. He was already prepared for one. In the meantime they had imperceptibly descended next to a new bridge on the Danube. It was primarily yellow and the lights on it seemed brighter than all the previous ones. The entire town was sparkling too. The Blue Bridge told him the name of the town without being asked.

He'd been wrong about the applause. It had been for the hairless dog after all, bowing to the audience on its hind legs on the railing. The smaller ragamuffin joined it, standing next to three thick books. The bird-dog looked in disbelief at the sheets of paper he was holding head-high. It seemed that all the pages were there. So how did he perform that sleight of hand with burning them, and more to the point, why did he do it at all? Well, no sense in racking his brain over it. Who could understand writers?

When the applause finally faded, the bigger homeless man picked up the little dog and put it back under his army coat. The smaller one put the sheets back in the folder and placed it under his coat too. Then both of them picked up the books, put them next to the suitcases and sat on them. The bird-dog hesitated briefly before joining the enlarged audience. He should not draw rash conclusions. Things were not always as they seemed with artists.

Just as the dog joined them, all eyes turned to the sliding doors that were opening. A motley procession began to embark from the Yellow Bridge. It was led by a gray-haired man in a raincoat with the collar turned up. He was followed by a short, overweight, bald fellow whose bright-red bow tie was all that disturbed the blackness of his clothes. An older man in a dark-blue pinstriped suit was holding a rope with a noose at the end. The solidly built middle-aged man behind him had large hands. The last to appear was a man with a Pekingese dog. He was holding it in his arms, whispering something to it, causing the dog to shake its little head and yap.

The bird-dog looked at the tiny dog in amusement. Of all dogs, he most despised well-groomed, pampered ones that served as drawing-room ornaments. It wouldn't survive half a day in nature or on the street. Even the wretched hairless one deserved more respect than this scented powder puff. And putting on such airs.

The five-member troupe headed to the place that served as a stage. They bowed and were given brief applause. Then the man with the Pekingese put his pet on the railing and spent a few minutes sprucing it up. He took a little comb and brush out of his shoulder bag and back-combed the long hair on its back. Then he fixed up its tail and finally wiped its little paws with a silk handkerchief. He took a step back, inspected the Pekingese, then went up to it and lightly kissed the tip of its little snout.

How touching, thought the bird-dog, barely holding back a howl.

The newcomers took long, flat little boxes made of fancy wood out of their inside pockets. They opened them and showed the audience what was inside, and received another round of applause. They were filled to the top with a dense substance resembling clay. Fingers scooped out the soft mass and soon there was a lump in each of the five pairs of hands, each one a different color: black, yellow, red, white and blue.

Turning their backs to the audience, the five of them made a semicircle around the Pekingese. They waited patiently for the Blue Bridge to soar above Vienna and then got down to work.

◅ 5 ◢

BITTERNESS CAME OVER THE bird-dog when he realized what they were doing. It was apparent even from
the back by the brisk movements of their hands and periodic raising their eyes to the Pekingese on the railing.
Here's more proof of what an unfair world this is! Why
should the sculptors use this flabby ball for a model?
He was much more suitable, all muscular, supple, slen-
der, elongated.

But who among decadent artists still values real
canine virtues? He immediately saw for himself that
these virtues were also unappreciated among the no
less decadent audience. The fascinated viewers were
clapping rhythmically, spurring on the sculptors who
quickened their movements as though competing to
see who would be the first to finish. The bird-dog felt
like moving away demonstratively again, but as he was
making up his mind, the five men turned in unison
and ovations echoed throughout the bridge.

Each sculptor proudly held his work before him.
Their faces were beaded in sweat, but also radiant. The
bird-dog stared at the little clay sculptures in bewilderment. It's a good thing I didn't pose, he thought with
relief. How would these nutty guys have represented
him when the Pekingese inspired them to sculpt little
bridges? Even though he still despised the dolled up
little dog, for a moment he felt sorry for it. No dog
deserves to be humiliated like that.

The little bridges were not ugly in themselves. On
the contrary, one might say. He would have liked
them if they hadn't come about under such circumstances. The sculptors had skillful fingers and the little models looked quite convincing, as though made

of metal and not clay. As a dog that had already seen the world, he easily recognized all the bridges except the black one.

What are they going to do with their works, wondered the bird-dog. They would be ruined if they tried to put them in the little boxes they'd placed on the pavement. But this concern did not plague the sculptors yet. Holding the bridges on their outstretched palms, they reached into their inside pockets with their free hand and took out an egg this time. The applause ceased the same moment.

Hands went up high and then smashed down on the top of their heads. The cracking of the eggshells was clearly heard in the silence. But the contents didn't end up on their heads because the sculptors quickly lowered their closed fists. Their fingers moved apart over the little bridges and the mixture of egg whites and yolks dribbled over the clay.

Is this some kind of technique to strengthen the clay and give it a shine, wondered the bird-dog. This was merely conjecture because he didn't understand a thing about the artisan side of sculpting. As they brought the bridges to their mouths, he naively thought they wanted to blow on them for some reason. He didn't suspect what would follow even when they opened their mouths. He finally had to accept the obvious when the little bridges began to enter their mouths.

Disgusted, the bird-dog quickly closed his eyes. He couldn't watch. Well, dogs weren't picky, they ate whatever they found when their stomach growled, but even a dog dying of hunger would never put clay covered with eggs in its mouth. Phooey! His stomach turned.

The rhythmical clapping that started again added irritation to his nausea. He didn't have to open his eyes to know what lay behind this new encouragement. The five perverse sculptors were competing to see who could devour their work first and the equally perverse audience was spurring them on.

This wouldn't have been so hard to take if he'd been in the midst of the ordinary rabble, but he never would have expected such behavior from artists. Who were dogs to look up to, whose example should they follow, if artists were no different from the rest? How dreadful. Moving away from this group was no longer enough. He would keep his eyes closed until they went down to the next bridge and then he would get off the Blue Bridge, wherever it was. This was no place for him.

Yes, but how would he know they'd got there when the halts were imperceptible? He raised his eyelids a tiny bit after the applause finally stopped. There had even been cheers at the high point. He dreaded what he would see, but it turned out to be nothing unseemly, so he opened his eyes all the way. The sculptors were closing the little wooden boxes full of clay.

What does this mean, wondered the bird-dog. Didn't they eat the little bridges? Had he closed his eyes too soon? Who knows what he'd missed if that was the case. He'd been rash again. It would be the death of him one day. Sheepishly, he watched the sculptors join the audience. The Pekingese's owner proudly petted his dog and it puffed up so much it almost burst.

They had landed next to the Black Bridge that seemed like a dwarf compared to the Blue Bridge, because here the Danube was not even half as wide as it was in Novi Sad. It was constructed solely of stone and must have been very old. At first the bird-dog thought its lighting was paler than on the other bridges, and then he realized what caused this impression. He turned to look toward the downstream side. The sky was turning red in the east. Day would soon break.

His eyes turned forward again because his sensitive ears had picked up the barely audible sound of the sliding doors. The passage between the two bridges was open, but several long moments passed before someone finally appeared. He was surprised to see just a dog instead of a new group of people.

Everything he felt about the Pekingese, if not worse, also held for white poodles. His hackles went up when he saw the dog head straight for him. It didn't seem the least bit threatening, which was a real shame. He would have preferred if it had. He'd been looking for a chance to show these conceited good-for-nothings what he thought about them.

On approaching, the poodle didn't address him. It just stood in front of him, wagging its tail. Before he had a chance to ask why it was goggling at him so obtusely, he heard something move on the left. The mongrel, hairless dog and Pekingese had emerged from the audience and were heading toward him as well.

They surrounded him and he braced, ready for action. Only the mongrel was a worthy opponent. All he had to do was growl at the other three. But none of them indicated any desire to attack him. On the contrary, now four tails were wagging. What do they want from me, wondered the bird-dog. Let them speak their minds for once. They can't stand there like that forever.

Applause broke up the standoff. Like a trained team, the four dogs ran to the railing. The Pekingese and poodle stood on the left side of the stage and the mongrel and hairless dog stood on the right. The bird-dog looked at them in bewilderment. What was going on? They didn't expect him to take part, did they?

The bird-dog's suspicions were confirmed when the clapping intensified, but he didn't move. This was impossible. He didn't have an act. He hadn't prepared anything. He would just make a fool of himself before these wonderful artists. He didn't move until the bridge silently told him to relax, everything would be all right. He had artistry of his own.

6

ONCE HE WAS ON the stage, the bird-dog was the first to hear what the others couldn't for lack of sharp ears. Somewhere below, near the surface of the Danube, was the barely audible flapping of birds' wings. The dog turned toward the railing behind him just as an enormous canvas started to appear above the bridge. It was being raised by a dozen river gulls holding the upper edge in their beaks.

Water was pouring off the painting without smearing the paint, rolling off like it was glass. He recognized what it depicted before it was even halfway visible.

Of course he recognized it, since he was standing on the Blue Bridge. He'd spent on it the whole of the previous night full of wonders.

The canvas stopped rising when the lower edge was level with the railing. It towered above the bird-dog and he had to throw his head way back to take it all in. Now he could absorb the details. The first thing that caught his eye was the gulls on the painting standing on the railing, looking at the same place beneath it. He was filled with a mixture of discomfort and pride when he realized that their eyes were trained on him. Indeed, he was painted from the back, but there was no doubt it was him.

The gulls holding the canvas let go of it in unison and flew away. But the painting didn't fall, hovering as though in an invisible frame. The dog watched the birds as they flew in a wide semicircle to the other side of the bridge. He was shocked when he realized what they were up to, but the audience was not alarmed, as though unaware or unconcerned.

The bird-dog started barking at the gulls, but this didn't stop them. Flying low in attack formation, they zeroed in on the canvas. For a moment he felt like closing his eyes, not wanting to see them rip through it, but the recollection of his previous rashness prevented him. What if his expectations were wrong again?

He cringed at the moment of impact, but was filled with immediate relief on seeing that the painting was unharmed. At first he couldn't figure out what had happened to the birds. They seemed to have disappeared. Then he stared in disbelief at the gulls on the painting that seemed to have come to life. They were still on the railing but were visibly moving. In addition, shrieking came from the painting.

The bird-dog was startled to feel the birds looking at him. They were no longer focused on his painted image. Their cries became louder as though calling to him. He looked at them in bewilderment. The same instant rhythmic clapping started up again behind him. He turned around. They were all on their feet, smiling at him. He shook his head. They'd greatly overrated him if they thought he was up to that.

Of course you're up to it, said the bridge to him soundlessly. Would I have brought you all the way to Regensburg otherwise?

Hesitating a bit longer, the bird-dog stepped back a little and then jumped onto the railing. That was easy.

The next jump compelled him to suppress the very foundations of his being—instincts, natural caution, fear—and have unlimited confidence in the bridge. To embrace the wonder.

He pushed off with his hind legs. For some reason he'd thought the crossing would take some time, even though the painting was right in front of him. It was over in an instant, however, as though he'd really just jumped from one Blue Bridge to another.

The dog was greeted by happy shrieking and then wings started fluttering and the gulls flew off. Cries came from somewhere down below. He looked through the railing at the world outside the painting. Standing next to each other, the Blue Bridge and the Black Bridge were now a little below the canvas that the flying birds were raising. The folks on the Blue Bridge waved goodbye to him. He replied with clumsy movements of his paws.

As the painting rose on the wings of the gulls, the Blue Bridge underneath it suddenly began to shine. The bird-dog first thought it was a trick of the dawning sun, but then the same thing would have happened to the Black Bridge and the surrounding area. Everything appeared stable but the bridge that had brought him there. It was losing its solidity and eroding, along with everyone on it.

What puzzled the dog even more than this mysterious phenomenon was the attitude of the people and the dogs. They kept on waving at him gaily as though everything was all right and they were not becoming thinner and paler. Not understanding anything, the bird-dog stood by the railing and watched in alarm as the bridge turned into a blue cloud low over the water.

When it had become completely amorphous, blue

powder began to fall from it in the form of the softest rain. It poured into the Danube, turning its turbid grayness into a diaphanous blue, as though the river were reflecting a clear sky. A blue ribbon swiftly began to flow upstream and downstream from the Black Bridge.

Watching it unwind in both directions, the dog suddenly realized what he had to do. A bird-dog's job is to chase birds, isn't it? That's why he'd been chosen for this undertaking. He started barking and the gulls obediently got into formation and flew toward the river on the painting that had also been draped in blue.

Following the movement of the birds on it, the canvas went down to just above the Danube and rushed toward the east. It soon reached the beginning of the ribbon and continued along with it, filling out taut like a sail. A thrill went through the bird-dog. A moment ago he'd been convinced that nothing could surpass the experience of the night's flight on the bridge, but it was nothing compared with sailing on the crest of a wave that was painting the great river blue like a giant paintbrush.

Under any other circumstances he would have preferred a slower voyage, but now was not the time to take in the wonderful landscape along the banks of the Danube. Before the sun rose he had to bring to an end what had begun the night before on the Blue Bridge. Now he was the only one left.

The bridges under which they passed greeted them euphorically. The bird-dog had no idea there were so many of them. Even the four he'd landed next to seemed like a lot. He would really have to start studying geography. He didn't have to learn about all four corners of the world exactly, but he certainly would learn about the Danube River basin.

The five sculptors and the Pekingese were waiting for him on the Yellow Bridge in Vienna. Quickly moving underneath them, he was briefly amused at the sight of a man on the deck of a tourist boat passing by. Thinking that the group on the bridge was waving at him, he waved back.

Two smiling homeless men were standing on the bank under the Red Bridge in Bratislava, each one holding three thick books. When the painting glided up to them, the hairless little dog stuck its head out of the army coat and cheerfully yapped. The bird-dog grumbled a greeting in return.

Even though the six musicians in the middle of the White Bridge in Budapest didn't have any instruments, festive music rang out when the blue wave reached them. The swaying mongrel on the railing seemed to be conducting an invisible orchestra.

The bird-dog would have loved to float down the Danube like this forever—with his ignorance of geography he imagined it to be a river that never ended anywhere—but they were quickly approaching the last stop on his great voyage. Although he was happy to return to Novi Sad, he felt a pang of sorrow when he barked the final order to the gulls.

In order to detach the canvas from the crest with which it seemed to have fused, they had to flap their wings fiercely that until then had only been spread. The painting soared above the Danube and the bird-dog gazed for a moment in admiration at the blue ribbon as it continued winding its way swiftly downstream.

But there was no more time for admiration. The sun that had been considerate enough to stay just above the eastern horizon to give them a chance to finish their undertaking outside of time would soon continue rising. Before this happened, the final act was left.

The gulls closed their wings and the canvas headed down to the river like an enormous cover. Had there been anyone on the quay at that early hour, they would have witnessed a wondrous transformation. But there were no eye-witnesses. Not only was it early, but the all-clear siren had yet to be sounded.

Sinking lower and lower, the canvas took on a new dimension. It ceased to be an image on a painting and took on a form in the real world. When it got within reach of the water, it was already in the shape of the Blue Bridge. As light as a feather even though it was very heavy, it touched the ground where it had flown away the night before and reconnected with the banks and two towers.

As soon as time started to course again, the gulls scattered in the sky. A long return flight to their own bridge awaited them. The bird-dog took off without a moment's hesitation too. He had nothing left to do there. People would soon be coming out of their shelters, and they were inquisitive creatures. They would gaze at not one but two wonders—an intact bridge and blue water under it—and would want an explanation. That was their natural tendency, something they couldn't get rid of, even though it was only to their detriment. Someone might even think of questioning him if he was the only one there. And what could he tell them? That what they were looking at was a mere trifle? That the great Danube was a river full of wonders? Would anyone believe him?

Contributors

About the author

Zoran Živković was born in Belgrade, Serbia, on October 5, 1948. Until his recent retirement, he was a full professor at the Faculty of Philology, the University of Belgrade, teaching creative writing. He is one of the most translated contemporary Serbian writers: by the end of 2019 there were more than 100 foreign editions of his books of fiction, published in 23 countries, in 20 languages.

Živković has won several literary awards for his fiction. In 1994 his novel *The Fourth Circle* won the Miloš Crnjanski award. In 2003, Živković's mosaic novel *The Library* won a World Fantasy Award for Best Novella. In 2007 his novel *The Bridge* won the Isidora Sekulić award. In 2007 Živković received the Stefan Mitrov Ljubiša award for his life achievement in literature. In 2014 and 2015 Živković received three awards for his contribution to the literature of fantastika: Art-Anima, Stanislav Lem and The Golden Dragon.

Živković is the author of 22 books of fiction:
    The Fourth Circle (1993)
    Time Gifts (1997)
    The Writer (1998)
    The Book (1999)
    Impossible Encounters (2000)
    Seven Touches of Music (2001)
    The Library (2002)
    Steps through the Mist (2003)
    Hidden Camera (2003)
    Compartments (2004)
    Four Stories till the End (2004)
    Twelve Collections and the Teashop (2005)
    The Bridge (2006)
    Miss Tamara, The Reader (2006),
    Amarcord (2007)
    The Last Book (2007)
    Escher's Loops (2008)
    The Ghostwriter (2009)
    The Five Wonders of the Danube (2011)
    The Grand Manuscript (2012)
    The Compendium of the Dead (2015)
    The Image Interpreter (2016)

About the artist

Youchan Ito was born 1968 in Aichi prefecture, Japan. She launched her career as a graphic designer in 1988, becoming a freelancer illustrator in 1991 and founding Togoru Co., Ltd. with her husband in 2000. In 2017 the company was reborn as Togoru Art Works. She works with a wide range of genres including cover art and design for science fiction, mysteries and horror titles, as well as illustrations for children's books.

www.youchan.com

.